BEFOR

(A MACKENZIE WHITE MYSTERY—BOOK 5)

BLAKE PIERCE

BOOKS BY BLAKE PIERCE

RILEY PAIGE MYSTERY SERIES
ONCE GONE (Book #1)
ONCE TAKEN (Book #2)
ONCE CRAVED (Book #3)
ONCE LURED (Book #4)
ONCE HUNTED (Book #5)
ONCE PINED (Book #6)
ONCE FORSAKEN (Book #7)
ONCE COLD (Book #8)
ONCE STALKED (Book #9)

MACKENZIE WHITE MYSTERY SERIES
BEFORE HE KILLS (Book #1)
BEFORE HE SEES (Book #2)
BEFORE HE COVETS (Book #3)
BEFORE HE TAKES (Book #4)
BEFORE HE NEEDS (Book #5)
BEFORE HE FEELS (Book #6)

AVERY BLACK MYSTERY SERIES
CAUSE TO KILL (Book #1)
CAUSE TO RUN (Book #2)
CAUSE TO HIDE (Book #3)
CAUSE TO FEAR (Book #4)

KERI LOCKE MYSTERY SERIES
A TRACE OF DEATH (Book #1)
A TRACE OF MUDER (Book #2)
A TRACE OF VICE (Book #3)

PROLOGUE

Joey Nestler knew that he'd make a good cop one day. His father had been a cop and so had his grandfather. Joey's grandfather had actually taken a bullet in the chest in 1968, sending him to early retirement. Being a cop was in Joey's blood and even though he was only twenty-eight years old and was being given crap assignments, he knew that one day he would rise to the top.

Today was not that day, though. They'd assigned him another stupid bait-and-chase task—grunt work. Joey knew he had at least another six months of these bullshit assignments. That was fine with him. Coasting through Miami in a cop car during late spring was a pretty sweet deal. The ladies were eager to try on their skimpy shorts and bathing suits as the weather got nicer, and such things were easier to pay attention to and enjoy when he was tasked with menial duties.

He'd get right back to scanning the streets for such beauties when he was done with his most recent chore. He parked in front of the ritzy townhouses, each new set of homes bordered by a pretentiously well-maintained set of palm trees. He got out of the patrol car in no great hurry, pretty sure he was about to walk into a simple domestic dispute case. Even so, he had to admit that the details of the assignment piqued his curiosity.

A woman had called the precinct earlier that morning, claiming that her sister was not answering phone calls or emails. Usually that would not draw much interest at all, but when they ran the address of the sister, it was directly beside a townhouse that had called with a noise complaint the night before. Apparently a dog had been barking furiously all night. Phone calls and knocks on the door to get the owners to shut up went unanswered. And when the police called the woman back to inquire about her sister, it was confirmed that her sister did indeed have a dog.

And now here I am, Joey thought as he walked up the stairs to the front door.

He'd already stopped by the landlord's office to retrieve a key, and that in and of itself made the task a *little* more interesting than his typical busy-body assignments. Still, he felt underused and a little silly as he knocked on the door. Given everything he knew about the case, he didn't even expect an answer.

He knocked again and again, his hair sweating beneath his cap in the sun.

After two minutes, still no answer. He was not surprised.

1

Joey took out the key and unlocked the door. He cracked it open a bit and shouted inside.

"Hello? This is Officer Nestler with the Miami PD. I'm entering the house and—"

The barking of a small dog interrupted him as it came rushing toward him. It was a Jack Russell terrier and while it tried its best to intimidate the strange man at the door, it also looked a little scared. Its back legs were trembling.

"Hey, buddy," Joey said as he stepped inside. "Where's your mommy and daddy?"

The little dog whined. Joey stepped further into the house. He had made two steps into the small foyer, heading for the living room, when he smelled the awful stench. He looked down to the dog and frowned.

"No one has let you out in a while, have they?"

The dog hung its head, as if it had perfectly understood the question and was ashamed of what it had done.

Joey walked into the living room, still calling out.

"Hello? I'm looking for Mr. or Mrs. Kurtz. Again, this is Officer Nestler of the Miami PD."

But he got no answer, and he was sure he wouldn't get one. He made his way through the living room, finding it spotless. He then entered the adjoining kitchen and placed his hand to his face to cover his mouth and nose. The kitchen was where the dog had decided to use the bathroom; puddles of urine were all over the floor and two piles of feces were in front of the fridge.

Empty food and water dishes were on the other side of the kitchen. Feeling bad for the dog, Nestler filled the water bowl with water from the kitchen sink. The dog started to lap at it greedily as Nestler left the kitchen. He then went to the flight of stairs just off of the living room and headed up.

As he came to the hallway at the top, Joey Nestler felt what his father had called *a cop's gut instinct* for the first time in his career. He knew right away that something was wrong up here. He knew that he was going to find something bad, something that he had not been expecting.

He drew his gun, feeling a little foolish as he made his way down the hallway. He passed a bathroom (where he found another puddle of the dog's urine) and a small office space. The office was a bit of a mess but there were no signs of distress or red flags.

At the end of the hall, a third and final door stood open, revealing the master bedroom.

Nestler stopped in the doorway, his blood running cold.

2

He stared for a full five seconds before stepping inside.

A man and a woman—presumably Mr. and Mrs. Kurtz—lay dead on the bed. He knew they were not sleeping due to the amount of blood on the sheets, walls, and carpet.

Joey took two steps inside but stopped. This was not for him. He needed to call this in before he went any further. Besides, he could see all he needed to from where he stood. Mr. Kurtz had been stabbed in the chest. Mrs. Kurtz had had her throat slit from ear to ear.

Joey had never seen so much blood in his life. It was almost dizzying to look at.

He backed out of the bedroom, not thinking of his father or grandfather, not thinking of the great cop he one day wanted to be.

He stormed outside, got to the bottom of the stairs, and fought against a heavy wave of nausea. As he fumbled for the shoulder mic on his uniform, he saw the Jack Russell come rushing out of the townhouse but didn't care.

He and the little dog stood in front of the house as Nestler called the scene in, the dog yapping at the sky as if somehow that could change the horrors that lay inside.

CHAPTER ONE

Mackenzie White sat at her cubicle and habitually ran her index finger along the edges of a business card. It was a business card that she had been fixated on for several months now, a card that was somehow linked to her past. Or, more specifically, to the murder of her father.

She came back to it whenever she closed a case, wondering when she would allow herself to take some time off from her actual job as an agent so she could return to Nebraska and view the scene of her father's death with reinvigorated eyes that were not regulated by an FBI mentality.

Work was burning her out lately and with each case she cracked, the lure of the mystery surrounding her father grew stronger. It was getting so strong that she was feeling less of a sense of accomplishment when she closed a case. The most recent had been bringing in two men that had been masterminding a plot to get cocaine into a Baltimore high school. The job had lasted three days and had gone so smoothly that it hadn't seemed like work at all.

She'd had more than her fair share of notable cases since coming to Quantico and being pushed through the ranks in a whirlwind of action, back-room dealings, and close calls. She'd lost a partner, managed to piss off just about every supervisor she'd ever had, and made a name for herself.

The one thing she didn't have was a friend. There was Ellington, sure, but there was some sort of tainted chemistry between them that made forming a friendship difficult. And she'd officially given up on him, anyway. He'd rejected her twice now— for different reasons each time—and she was not going to be made a fool of again. She was fine with their working relationship being the only thread holding them together.

Over the last few weeks, she had also gotten to know her knew partner—a clumsy but eager rookie by the name of Lee Harrison. He was being handed an assortment of paperwork, busy duty, and research, but he was doing a splendid job. She knew that Director McGrath was just seeing how he'd handle being inundated with so much busywork. And so far, Harrison was winning everyone over.

She thought faintly of Harrison as she looked at the business card. She had asked him on a few occasions to research any businesses called Barker Antiques. And while he had come up with more results than anyone else in the last few months, all leads had still come to a dead end.

As she thought about this, she heard soft footsteps approaching her cubicle. Mackenzie slid the business card under a pile of papers beside her laptop and then pretended like she was checking her email.

"Hey, White," a familiar male voice said.

The guy is so good that he can practically hear me thinking about him, she thought. She swiveled around in her chair and looked at Lee Harrison peering into her cubicle.

"None of this *White,* stuff," she said. "It's Mackenzie. Mac, if you're feeling really brave."

He smiled awkwardly. It was clear that Harrison had not yet figured out how to speak to her or, for that matter, how to really even act around her. And that was fine with her. Sometimes she wondered if McGrath had assigned him as her sometimes-partner just to get him accustomed to never being sure where he stood with his coworkers. If so, she thought, it was a genius move.

"Okay then...Mackenzie," he said. "I just wanted you to know that they've just finished processing the dealers from this morning. They want to know if you need any more information from them."

"Nope. I'm good," she said.

Harrison nodded but before he left, he gave her a frown that she was starting to think was a trademark of his. "Can I ask you something?" he asked.

"Of course."

"Are you...well, are you feeling all right? You look really tired. Maybe a little flushed."

She could have easily ribbed him about such a comment and made him very awkward but she decided not to. He was a good agent and she didn't want to be the sort of agent (really not much more than a rookie herself) that hassled the new guy. So instead, she said: "Yeah, I'm good. Just not sleeping much lately."

Harrison nodded. "I get that," he said. "Well...good luck with resting." He then gave that trademark frown of his and took off, probably on to tackle whatever busybody work McGrath had lined up for him next.

Distracted from the business card and the countless unsolved mysteries it presented, Mackenzie allowed herself to leave it behind. She caught up on her emails and filed away some of the papers that had started collecting on her desk. She did not get many chances to experience these less-than-glamorous moments, and for that, she was thankful.

When her phone rang in the midst of it all, she grabbed for it anxiously. *Anything to get away from this desk.*

5

"This is Mackenzie White," she answered.

"White, it's McGrath."

She allowed the briefest of smiles to cross her face. While McGrath was far from her favorite person, she knew that whenever he called her up or even came by her cubicle, it was usually with an assignment of some sort.

It appeared that this was why he was calling. Mackenzie didn't even have time to say hello before he was speaking again, in his usual rapid-fire way of communicating.

"I need you in my office right away," he said. "And bring Harrison with you."

Again, Mackenzie was not given a chance to respond. The line was dead before a single word could bounce from her tongue.

But that was fine with her. Apparently, McGrath had a new case for her. Maybe it would sharpen her mind and give her that one last moment of clarity before she possibly stepped aside for a while to concentrate on matters with her father's old case.

With a bubbling sort of excitement pushing her, she got up and went off in search of Lee Harrison.

***

Watching the way Harrison behaved in McGrath's office was a great way for Mackenzie to ground herself. She watched him sitting rigidly at the edge of his seat as McGrath started speaking to them. The younger agent was clearly nervous and eager to please. Mackenzie knew that he was a perfectionist and that he had something very close to a photographic memory. She wondered what his memory was like—if he was perhaps soaking up each word that came out of McGrath's mouth like a sponge.

He reminds me a little bit of me, she thought as she also focused on McGrath.

"Here's what I've got for the two of you," McGrath said. "Yesterday morning, the Miami State Police called us up and filled us in on a series of murders down there. In both cases, the murders were of married couples. So that's four bodies. The murders have been fairly brutal and bloody and so far, there seems to be no obvious connection. The brutal style of the killings, as well as the fact that they were married couples, killed in bed, is making the state PD down there think it's a serial killer. I personally think it's too early to make such a claim."

"You think it could just be coincidence?" Mackenzie asked.

"I think it's a chance, yes," he said. "Anyway, they've asked for our help and I want to send both of you down. Harrison, this would be a great opportunity for you to get into the field and get your feet wet. White, I expect you to oversee him, but not boss him around. Got it?"

"Yes, sir," Mackenzie said.

"I'll have the details and flight arrangements sent your way within the hour. I don't see this taking any more than a day or two. Any questions?"

Mackenzie shook her head. Harrison gave a brisk "No sir," and Mackenzie could tell that he was doing his very best to rein in his excitement.

She couldn't blame him. She felt it, too.

Despite what McGrath thought, she already sensed this case would be far from routine.

Couples.

This was a first for her.

And she could not help but feel that this "routine" little case was going to get far worse.

CHAPTER TWO

While Mackenzie was well aware that a stereotype of the government was that everything moved slowly, she also knew that this was not usually the case with the FBI getting their agents on the scene. Just fourteen hours after being called into McGrath's office, Mackenzie was pulling a rental car into a parking spot in front of a row of townhouses. She pulled in next to a police cruiser and took note of the officer sitting inside.

Beside her, in the passenger seat, Harrison was going over the notes on the case. He had been mostly quiet during the trip and Mackenzie had nearly started to try to open up the lines of conversation. She couldn't tell if he was nervous, intimidated, or a bit of both. But rather than force him to start speaking to her, she thought it might be best for his development to come out of his shell on his own—especially if McGrath planned on them working together as partners for the foreseeable future.

Mackenzie took a moment to process everything she knew about the case. She reclined her head back slightly, closed her eyes, and pulled it all forward. Her tendency toward obsessing over the details of case files made it rather easy for her to simply delve into her own mind and rifle through them as if there were a mental filing cabinet within her skull.

A dead couple, which brings a few questions to the surface right away. Why both of them? Why not just one?

Got to keep an eye out for anything that might seem even remotely out of place. If jealousy is driving these killings, it's likely from someone that envies their lives in some way.

No forced entry; the Kurtz family willingly let the killer inside.

She opened her eyes and then opened the door. She could speculate all she wanted based on what she had seen in the files. But none of that would be as effective as stepping foot into the crime scene and having a look around.

Harrison stepped out of the car alongside her and into the bright Miami sunshine. She could smell the ocean in the air, salty and with just the faintest traces of a fishlike smell that wasn't necessarily unpleasant.

As she and Harrison closed their doors, the officer in the police car next to them also stepped out. This, Mackenzie assumed, was the officer who had been tasked with meeting them. Forty or so, she looked pretty in a plain sort of way, her short dirty blonde hair catching the shine from the sun.

8

"Agents White and Harrison?" the officer asked.

"That's us," Mackenzie said.

The woman offered her hand as she introduced herself. "I'm Officer Dagney," she said. "Anything you need, just let me know. The place has, of course, been cleaned up but I've got a whole file filled with pictures taken when the scene was fresh."

"Thanks," Mackenzie said. "To start off, I think I'd like to take a look inside first."

"Of course," Dagney said, walking up the stairs and retrieving a key from her pocket. She unlocked the door and gestured for Mackenzie and Harrison to step inside ahead of her.

Mackenzie smelled bleach or some other sort of cleaner right away. She recalled the report stating that a dog had been trapped inside the house for at least two days and had used the bathroom several times.

"The bleach," Harrison said. "Is that from cleaning up the dog's mess?"

"Yes," Dagney said. "That was done last night. We tried to leave it as it was until you guys arrived but the stench was just—it was bad."

"That should be fine," Mackenzie said. "The bedroom is upstairs, correct?"

Dagney nodded and led them up the stairs. "The only thing that's been changed up here is that the bodies and the top sheet have been removed," she explained. "The sheet is still there, on the floor and placed on a plastic sheet. It had to be moved, though, just to get the bodies off of the bed. The blood was…well, you'll see."

Mackenzie noticed that Harrison slowed his approach a bit, falling safely in behind her. Mackenzie followed Dagney to the bedroom door, noticing that she stayed at the doorway and did everything she could not to look inside.

Once she was inside the room, Mackenzie saw that Dagney had not exaggerated, nor had the reports she had read. There was a lot of blood—much more than she had ever seen at one site.

And for a horrifying moment, she was standing in a room in Nebraska—a room in a house she knew was now abandoned. She was looking at a blood-soaked bed that contained the body of her father.

She shook the image away at the sound of Harrison's footsteps slowly approaching behind her.

"You good?" she asked him.

"Yeah," he said, though his voice sounded a bit breathless.

9

Mackenzie noted that most of the blood was on the bed, as was expected. The sheet that had been removed from the bed and stretched out on the floor had once been an off-white. But now it was mostly covered in dried blood, going a rusty shade of maroon. She slowly approached the bed, pretty sure that there would be no evidence. Even if the killer had accidentally left behind a hair or anything with DNA, it would be buried in all of the blood.

She looked to the splatters on the wall and carpet. She eyed the carpet in particular, looking to see if any of the blood splatter could be the edge of a shoe.

There might be tracks of some kind, she thought. *To kill someone in such a way—to have so much blood at the scene—the killer would* have *to have gotten some on him. So even if there are no tracks, maybe there's stray blood somewhere within the house, blood he might have accidentally left behind on his way out.*

Also, how did the killer get them both while in bed? Killing one, the other would have likely woken up. Either the killer is that fast or he staged the scene with the bodies in bed after committing the murders.

"This is a mess, huh?" Harrison said.

"It is," Mackenzie said. "Tell me…do you see anything right off hand that you'd consider a lead, a clue, or anything to look deeper into?"

He shook his head, staring at the bed. She nodded in agreement, knowing that all of the blood would make it very hard to find any evidence. She even got down on her hands and knees, peering under the bed to see if there was anything under there. She saw nothing but a pair of slippers and an old photo album. She slid the album out and flipped through it. The first few pages showed a wedding, from the bride walking down the aisle of a large church to the happy couple cutting into their cake.

With a frown, she slid the album back where she had gotten it from. She then turned back to Dagney, still standing at the bedroom door with her back mostly turned. "You said you have files with photos, right?"

"I do. Give me a second and I can bring it all in." She answered quickly and with a bit of urgency, clearly anxious to get back downstairs.

When Dagney was gone, Harrison walked back out into the hallway. He looked back into the bedroom and sighed deeply. "Have you ever seen a crime scene like this?"

"Not with this much blood," she answered. "I've seen some grisly sites, but this one tops the list for amount of blood."

10

Harrison seemed to think hard about this as Mackenzie exited the room. They headed back downstairs together, stepping into the living room just as Dagney came back in the front door. They met at the bar area that separated the kitchen from the living room. Dagney placed the folder on the bar and Mackenzie opened it up. Right away, the first picture showed the same bed upstairs, coated in blood. Only in the picture, there were two bodies—a man and a woman. The Kurtzes.

Both of them were clothed in what Mackenzie assumed was what they wore to bed. Mr. Kurtz (Josh, according to the reports) was wearing a T-shirt and a pair of boxers. Mrs. Kurtz (Julie) was wearing a spaghetti-strapped tank top and a pair of skimpy gym shorts. There were a variety of photographs, some taken so close to the bodies that Mackenzie caught herself cringing a few times. The photo of Mrs. Kurtz's sliced neck was particularly gruesome.

"I didn't see any positive ID on the weapon used within the reports," Mackenzie said.

"That's because no one had figured it out. Everyone just assumed a knife."

A very big knife, at that, Mackenzie thought as she tore her eyes away from the body of Mrs. Kurtz.

She saw that apparently, even in death, Mrs. Kurtz had reached out for the comfort of her husband. Her right hand was draped almost lazily across his thigh. There was something very sweet about it but it also broke her heart a little.

"And what about the first couple that was killed?" Mackenzie asked.

"That was the Sterlings," Dagney said, pulling several pictures and sheets of paper from the back of the folder.

Mackenzie looked at the pictures and saw a scene similar to what she had seen in the previous photos, as well as upstairs. A couple, lying in bed, blood everywhere. The only difference was that the husband in the Sterling photos had either been sleeping in the nude or had had his clothes removed by the killer.

These scenes are far too similar, Mackenzie thought. *It's almost as if they were staged.* She looked over the similarities, looking back and forth between the Kurtz and Sterling photos.

The bravery and sheer will to kill two people at once—and in such a brutal way. This guy is incredibly driven. Very motivated. And apparently not opposed to extreme violence.

"Correct me if I'm wrong," Mackenzie said, "but the Miami PD are working under the assumption that these were routine home invasions, correct?"

"Well, we were at first," Dagney said. "But from what we can tell, there are no signs of looting or theft. And since this is the second couple to be killed in the last week, it seems less and less likely they were simple home invasions."

"I'd agree with that," she said. "What about links between the two couples?" Mackenzie asked.

"So far nothing has come up, but we've got a team working on it."

"And with the Sterlings, were there any signs of a struggle?"

"No. Nothing."

Mackenzie again looked back down at the pictures and two similarities jumped out at her at once. One of them in particular made her skin crawl.

Mackenzie glanced back at the Kurtz photos. She saw the wife's hand resting dead on her husband's thigh.

And she knew right then: this was indeed the work of a serial killer.

CHAPTER THREE

Mackenzie followed behind Dagney as she led them to the station. On the way, she noticed that Harrison was jotting notes down in the folder he had practically obsessed over during most of the trip from DC to Miami. In the midst of writing, he paused and looked at her quizzically.

"You've already got a theory, don't you?" he asked.

"No. I don't have a theory, but I did notice a few things in the images that seemed a little odd to me."

"Want to share?"

"Not just yet," Mackenzie said. "If I have to go over it now and then again with the police, I'll reanalyze myself. Give me some time to sort through it all."

With a grin, Harrison returned to his notes. He did not complain that she was keeping things from him (which she wasn't) and he didn't press any further. He was doing his best to stay obedient and effective at the same time and she appreciated that.

On the ride to the precinct, she started to catch peeks of the ocean through some of the buildings they passed. She had never been enamored with the sea the way some people were but she could understand its draw. Even now, on the hunt for a killer, she could feel the sense of freedom it represented. Punctuated by the towering palm trees and flawless sun of a Miami afternoon made it even more beautiful.

Ten minutes later, Mackenzie followed Dagney into the parking lot of a large police building. Like just about everything else in the city, it had a beachy sort of feel. Several huge palm trees stood along the thin strip of lawn in front of the building. The simple architecture also managed to convey a relaxed yet refined feel. It was a welcoming place, a sensation that held up even after Mackenzie and Harrison were inside.

"There are only going to be three people, including myself, on this," Dagney said as she led them down a spacious hallway. "Now that you guys are here, my supervisor is going to likely take a very hands-off approach."

Good, Mackenzie thought. *The least amount of rebuttals and arguments, the better.*

Dagney led them into a small conference room at the end of the hallway. Inside, two men sat down at a table. One of them was hooking a projector up to a MacBook. The other was typing something furiously into a smart pad.

They both looked up when Dagney led them into the room. When they did, Mackenzie got the usual look…one she was getting tired of yet used to. It was a look that seemed to say: *Oh, a rather good-looking woman. I wasn't expecting that.*

Dagney made a quick round of introduction as Mackenzie and Harrison sat down at the table. The man with the smart pad was Police Chief Rodriguez, a grizzled old man with deep lines in his tanned face. The other man was a fairly new guy, Joey Nestler. Nestler, as it turned out, was the officer who had discovered the bodies of the Kurtzes. As he was introduced, he finished successfully hooking the monitor to the laptop. The projector shone a bright white light on a small screen attached to the wall in front of the room.

"Thanks for coming out," Rodriguez said, setting his pad aside. "Look, I'm not going to be that typical local police dick that gets in the way. You tell me what you need and if it's within reason, you'll get it. In return, I just ask that you help wrap it up quickly and not turn the city into a circus while you do it."

"It sounds like we want the same things, then," Mackenzie said.

"So, Joey here has all of the existing documents we have on this case," he said. "The coroner's reports just came in this morning and told us just what we expected. The Kurtzes were cut up and bled out. No drugs in their system. Totally clean. So far we have no discernable links between the two crimes. So if you have any ideas, I'd like to hear them."

"Officer Nestler," Mackenzie said, "do you have all of the crime scene photos from both sites?"

"I do," he said. He reminded Mackenzie a lot of Harrison— anxious, a little nervous, and visibly seeking to please his superiors and coworkers.

"Could you pull up the full body shots side by side and put them on the screen, please?" Mackenzie asked.

He worked quickly and had the images up on the projector screen, side by side, within ten seconds. Seeing the images in such a bright light in a semi-darkened room was eerie. Not wanting to let those in the room dwell on the severity of the pictures and lose focus, Mackenzie got right to the point.

"I think it's safe to say that these murders were not the result of a typical break-in or home invasion. Nothing was stolen and, in fact, there is no clear indication of a break-in of any kind. There aren't even any signs of a struggle. That means that whoever killed them was likely invited in or, at the very least, had a key. And the murders had to have happened quickly. Also, the absence of blood anywhere else within the house makes it appear that the murders happened in the bedroom—that there was no foul play anywhere else within the house."

Speaking it out loud helped her understand how strange it seemed.

The guy was not only invited in, but apparently invited into the bedroom. That means that the likelihood that he was actually invited is a small one. He had a key. Or knew where a spare one was located.

She went on before she derailed herself with new thoughts and projections.

"I want to look at these pictures because there are two odd things that stand out to me. First…look at how all four of them are lying perfectly flat on their back. Their legs are relaxed and well-postured. It's almost as if they were staged to look that way. And then there's one other thing—and if we're dealing with a serial killer, I think this might be the most important thing to note. Look at Mrs. Kurtz's right hand."

She gave the other four people in the room the chance to look. She wondered if Harrison would notice what she was getting at and blurt it out. She gave them three seconds or so and when no one said anything, she carried on.

"Her right hand is resting on her husband's thigh. It's the one part of her body that is not perfectly laid out. So either this is a coincidence or the killer *did* place their bodies in this position, purposefully moving her hand."

"So what if he did?" Rodriguez asked. "What's the point?"

"Well, now look at the Sterlings. Look at the husband's left hand."

This time she did not make it three seconds. It was Dagney who saw what she was referencing. And when she answered, her voice was thin and on edge.

"He's reaching out and placing his hand on his wife's thigh," she said.

"Exactly," Mackenzie said. "If it were just one of the couples, I would not even mention it. But that same gesture is present with both of these couples, making it evident that the killer did it with some intention."

"But for what?" Rodriguez asked.

"Symbolism?" Harrison suggested.

"It could be," Mackenzie said.

"But that's not really much to go on, is it?" Nestler asked.

15

"Not at all," Mackenzie said. "But at least it's *something*. If it's symbolic to the killer, there's a reason for it. So here's where I'd like to start: I'd like to get a list of suspects that have been recently paroled for violent crimes that were linked to home invasions. I still don't think it was a home invasion per se, but it's the most plausible place to start."

"Okay, we can get that for you," Rodriguez said. "Anything else?"

"Nothing just yet. Our next course of action is to speak with the family, friends, and neighbors of the couples."

"Yeah, we spoke to the Kurtzes' next of kin—a brother, sister, and a pair of parents. You're more than welcome to go back to them, but they didn't offer up much of anything. The brother of Josh Kurtz said that as far as he knew, they had a great marriage. The only time they fought was during football season when the Seminoles played the Hurricanes."

"What about the neighbors?" Mackenzie asked.

"We spoke with them, too. But it was brief. Mostly about the noise complaint they filed about the yapping dog."

"So that's where we'll start," Mackenzie said, looking over to Harrison.

And without another word, they stood and were out the door.

CHAPTER FOUR

Mackenzie found it a little unsettling to revisit the townhouses. While standing in the beautiful weather as they approached the neighbors' house, the knowledge that there was a bed in the next townhouse over that was coated in blood seemed surreal. Mackenzie suppressed a shudder and looked away from the Kurtzes' townhouse.

As she and Harrison made their way up the stairs to the neighbors' front door, Mackenzie's phone dinged, letting her know that she had received a text message. She pulled out the phone and saw that the text was from Ellington. She rolled her eyes as she read it.

How's the rookie working out for you? Miss me yet?

She nearly responded but didn't want to encourage him. She also didn't want to seem aloof or distracted in front of Harrison. She knew it was a conceited thing to think, but she was pretty sure he was looking to her as an example of sorts. Given that, she tucked her phone back into her pocket and walked up to the front door. She allowed Harrison to knock and he even did that with great caution and care.

Several seconds later, a flustered-looking woman answered the door. She looked to be in her mid-forties. She was dressed in a loose-fitting tank top and a pair of shorts that may as well have been nothing more than panties. She looked like she was probably a regular at the beach, and had obviously been to a plastic surgeon for her nose and possibly her breasts.

"Can I help you?" she asked.

"Are you Demi Stiller?"

"I am. Why?"

Mackenzie flashed her badge with an expert swiftness that she was getting much better at. "We're agents White and Harrison with the FBI. We were hoping to speak with you about your neighbors."

"That's fine, I guess," Demi said. "But we already spoke to the police."

"I know," Mackenzie said. "I was hoping to go a bit deeper. As I understand it, there was some frustration over the dog next door when they spoke to you."

"Yeah, there was," Demi said, ushering them in and closing the door behind them. "Of course, I had no idea that they had been killed when I made that call."

"Of course," Mackenzie said. "We're not here about that, anyway. We were hoping you might be able to give us some insights into their lives. Did you know them at all?"

Demi had led them to the kitchen, where Mackenzie and Harrison took a seat at the bar. The place was laid out just like the Kurtz residence. Mackenzie saw Harrison looking skeptically toward the stairs off of the adjoined living room.

"We weren't friends, if that's what you're asking," Demi said. "We'd say hi if we saw one another, you know? We grilled out on the back patio with them a few times, but that's about it."

"How long were they your neighbors?" Harrison asked.

"A little more than four years, I guess."

"And would you consider them good neighbors?" Mackenzie followed up.

Demi gave a little shrug. "For the most part. They had some noisy get-togethers here and there during football season but it wasn't too bad. I honestly almost didn't even call in the complaint about the stupid dog. The only reason I did is because no one answered the door over there when I knocked."

"I don't suppose you know if they ever had any regular guests, do you?"

"I don't think so," Demi said. "The cops asked the same sort of thing. My husband and I thought it over and I don't ever remember seeing any cars parked over there regularly unless it was their own."

"Well, do you know if they were involved in anything that might get us some people to talk to? Any sort of clubs or weird interests?"

"Not that I know of," Demi said. As she spoke, she was looking at the wall, as if trying to see through it and into the Kurtzes' townhouse. She looked a little sad, either for the loss of the Kurtzes or simply to have been dragged into the middle of this.

"You're certain?" Mackenzie pushed.

"Pretty certain, yeah. I think the husband played racquetball. I saw him going in a few times, just coming back from the gym. As for Julie, I don't know. I know she liked to draw but that's only because she showed me some of her stuff one time. But other than that…no. They pretty much stayed to themselves."

"Is there anything else about them—anything *at all*—that stands out to you?"

"Well," Demi said, still looking at the wall, "I know it's sort of lewd, but it was quite evident to my husband and me that the Kurtzes had quite an active sex life. The walls here are apparently thin—or the Kurtzes were very loud. I can't even tell you how many times we heard them. Sometimes it wasn't even just like muffled noises; they would be going *at it*, you know?"

"Anything violent?" Mackenzie asked.

"No, it never sounded like it," Demi said, now looking a little embarrassed. "They were just very enthusiastic. It was something we always wanted to complain to them about but never did. It's sort of embarrassing to bring it up, you know?"

"Sure," Mackenzie said. "You've mentioned your husband a few times. Where is he?"

"At work. He works a nine to five. I stay here and run a part-time editorial service, a work from home deal."

"Would you please ask him the same things I've asked you just to make sure I get all the possible information?" Mackenzie asked.

"Yes, of course."

"Thank you very much for your time, Mrs. Stiller. I may call you a little later if any other questions arise."

"That's fine," Demi said as she led them back toward the front door.

When they were outside and Demi Stiller had closed the door, Harrison looked back to the townhouse that Josh and Julie Kurtz had once called home. "So all we took away from that was the knowledge that they had a great sex life?" he asked.

"Seems like it," she said. "But that tells us that they had a strong marriage, perhaps. Add that to the statements from the family about their picture-perfect marriage and it makes it more challenging to find a reason for their murders. Or, on the other hand, it could be easier now. If they had a good marriage and stayed out of trouble, finding someone with something against them could prove to be easier. Now…take a look at your notes. Where would you choose to look next?"

Harrison seemed a little surprised that she had asked the question but he dutifully looked down at the notebook he kept his notes and files in. "We need to check out the first crime scene—the Sterling residence. The parents of the husband live six miles from the house, so it may be worth checking in with them."

"Sounds good to me," she said. "You got the addresses?"

She tossed him the car keys and headed for the passenger door. She took a moment to admire the look of surprise and pride on his face at the simple gesture as he caught the keys.

"Then lead the way," she said.

CHAPTER FIVE

The Sterling residence was eleven miles away from the Kurtzes' townhouse. Mackenzie couldn't help but admire the place as Harrison pulled into the long concrete driveway. The house sat about fifty yards off of the main road, lined with a gorgeous flowerbed and tall thin trees. The house itself was very modern, mostly comprised of windows and distressed wooden beams. It looked like an idyllic yet expensive home for a well-to-do couple. The only thing that broke this illusion was the strip of yellow crime scene tape strung along the front door.

When they started walking toward the front door, Mackenzie noted just how quiet the place was. It was blocked off from the other high-priced neighboring houses by a thick grove of trees, a lush wall of green that looked just as well maintained and expensive as the houses along this stretch of the city. While the property was not on the beach, she could hear it murmuring somewhere in the distance.

Mackenzie ducked under the crime scene tape and dug out the spare key that Dagney had provided from the Miami PD's original investigation. They stepped into a large foyer and Mackenzie was again taken aback by the absolute silence of everything. She took a look around at the layout of the house. A hallway stretched out to their left and ended in a kitchen. The rest of the house was quite open; a living room and large sitting area connected to one another, leading further off and out of sight toward a glassed-in back porch.

"What do we know about what happened here?" Mackenzie asked Harrison. She, of course, already knew. But she wanted to let him display his own smarts and commitment, hoping he would quickly get comfortable before the case really took off.

"Deb and Gerald Sterling," Harrison said. "He was thirty-six and she was thirty-eight. Killed in their bedroom in the same manner as the Kurtzes, though these murders took place at least three days before the Kurtz murders. Their bodies were discovered by their maid just after eight o'clock in the morning. The coroner's reports indicate that they had been killed the night before. Initial investigation's turned up absolutely no evidence of any kind, although forensics is currently analyzing hair fibers found clinging to the front door frame."

Mackenzie nodded along as he recited the facts. She was studying the downstairs, trying to get a feel for the sort of people the Sterlings were before heading up to the room where they had been killed. She passed by a large built-in bookshelf between the living room and sitting area. Most of the books were fiction, mostly by King, Grisham, Child, and Patterson. There were also a few art-related books. In other words, basic filler books that gave no insights into the personal lives of the Sterlings.

A decorative roll-top desk sat against the wall in the sitting area. Mackenzie lifted the top and looked inside but there was nothing of interest—just pens, paper, a few pictures, and other household debris.

"Let's go on up," she said.

Harrison nodded and took a deep, shaky breath.

"It's okay," Mackenzie said. "The Kurtz house got to me, too. But trust me...these sorts of situations *do* get easier."

You know that might not necessarily be a good thing, right? she thought to herself. *How many terrible sights have you become desensitized to ever since coming across that first woman on a post in the cornfields of Nebraska?*

She shook the thought away as she and Harrison reached the top of the stairs. The upstairs consisted of a long hallway that housed only three rooms. A large office sat to the left. It was tidy to the point of being almost empty, looking out into the grove of trees along the back of the house. The huge bathroom boasted his and hers sinks, a large shower, a tub, and a linen closet that was as large as Mackenzie's kitchen.

Just like downstairs, there was nothing to paint an accurate picture of the Sterlings or why anyone would want to kill them. Wasting no more time, Mackenzie walked toward the end of the hallway where the bedroom door was standing open. Sunlight came pouring in through a large window on the left side of the room. The light swallowed up the end of the bed, turning the maroon there an alarming shade of red.

It was dizzying in a way, to step into the bedroom of a spotless house to see all of the blood on the bed. The floor was hardwood but Mackenzie could see splatters of blood here and there. There was not as much blood on the walls here as they had seen at the Kurtz residence, but there was some speckled in droplets like some morbid abstract painting.

There was a faint smell like copper in the air, the scent of spilled blood having dried. It was faint but seemed to fill the room. Mackenzie walked around the edge of the bed, looking at the light gray sheets that had been deeply stained in red. She saw a single mark in the top sheet that might have been a puncture wound from the knife. She observed it closer and found that was exactly what she was looking at.

With a single lap around the bed, Mackenzie was sure that there was nothing here that would push the case along any further. She looked elsewhere around the room—the bedside tables, the dresser drawers, and the small entertainment center—looking for even the smallest detail.

She saw a slight indentation in the wall, no larger than a quarter. But there was speck of blood around it. There was more blood beneath it, a slight dribble that had dried on the wall and the smallest little fleck of it on the carpet beneath the indention.

She went to the indentation in the wall and looked at it closely. It was a peculiar shape, and the fact that there was blood centered around it made her think one was the result of the other. She stood up straight and checked the small hole's alignment with her body. She raised her arm slightly and bent it. In doing so, her elbow aligned with the hole almost perfectly.

"What have you got?" Harrison asked.

"Signs of a struggle, I believe," she answered.

He joined her and took note of the indentation. "Not much to go on, is it?" he asked.

"No, not really. But the blood makes it notable. That and the fact that this house is in pristine condition. It makes me think the killer did everything he could do hide any signs of a struggle. He almost staged the house, in a way. But this sign of a struggle could not be hidden."

She looked down at the small blood splotch on the carpet. It was faded and there were even very faint traces of red around it.

"See," she said, pointing. "Right there, it looks like someone tried cleaning this up. But he was either hurried or this last little bit just would not come up."

"Maybe we should double-check the Kurtz house then."

"Maybe," she agreed, although she felt confident that she had thoroughly looked the place over.

She stepped away from the wall and went to the enormous walk-in closet. She looked inside and saw more tidiness.

She did see the one single thing that could have been considered as messy within the entire house, though. A shirt and a pair of pants were crumpled up, pushed almost against the closet wall. She pulled the shirt away from the pants and saw that they were men's clothing—perhaps the last clothes that Gerald Sterling had ever worn.

Taking a chance, she reached into each of the front pockets. In one, she found seventeen cents in change. In the other, she found a crumpled receipt. She straightened it out and saw that it was from a grocery store five days ago…the last day of his life. She looked at the receipt and started to think.

How else can we discover what they did on their last days alive? Or the last week, or even month?

"Harrison, in those reports, didn't the Miami PD state that they had gone through the phones of the deceased to check for any red flags?"

"That's correct," Harrison said as he cautiously stepped around the bloody bed. "Contacts, incoming and outgoing calls, emails, downloads, everything."

"But nothing like Internet search history or anything like that?"

"No, not that I recall."

Placing the receipt back into the pair of jeans, Mackenzie exited the closet and then the bedroom. She headed back downstairs, aware that Harrison was following behind her.

"What is it?" Harrison asked.

"A hunch," she said. "A *hope,* maybe."

She walked back to the roll-top desk in the sitting area and opened it again. In the back, there was a small basket. A few pens stuck out, as did a basic single-sheet personal checkbook. *If they keep a house this tidy, I'd assume their checkbook is in the same condition.*

She took the checkbook out and found that she was correct. The figures were kept with meticulous care. Each transaction was written very legibly and with as much detail as possible. Even ATM withdrawals were accounted for. It took her about twenty seconds to realize that this checkbook was for some sort of secondary account and not for the Sterlings' primary checking. At the time of their death, the account held a little over seven thousand dollars.

She looked through the check register for anything that might give her some sort of clues but nothing jumped out at her. She did, however, see a few abbreviations that did not recognize. Most of the transactions for these entries were for amounts of around sixty to two hundred dollars. One of the entries she did not recognize had been written out for two thousand dollars.

While nothing in the register seemed immediately curious, she remained hung up on the abbreviations and initials that she was not familiar with. She snapped a few pictures of those entries with her phone and then returned the checkbook.

"You have an idea or something?" Harrison asked.

"Maybe," she said. "Could you please get Dagney on the phone and ask her to task someone with pulling up the Sterlings' financial records over the last year? Checking accounts, credit cards, even PayPal if they used it."

"Absolutely," Harrison said. He instantly pulled out his phone to complete the task.

I might not mind working with him so much after all, Mackenzie thought.

She listened to him speaking with Dagney while she closed the roll-top desk and looked back toward the stairs.

Someone walked up those stairs four nights ago and killed a married couple, she thought, trying to envision it. *But why? And again, why were there no signs of forced entry?*

The answer was simple: *Just like with the Kurtzes, the killer was invited in. And that means that they either knew who the killer was and let him in or the killer was playing a certain part...acting like someone they knew or someone in need.*

The theory felt flimsy but she knew there was something to it. If nothing else, it created a fragile link between the two couples.

And for now, that was enough of a connection to go on.

CHAPTER SIX

While she had been hoping to avoid speaking to the families of the recently deceased, Mackenzie found herself working her way down her to-do list faster than she had expected. After leaving the Sterlings' house behind, the next natural place to go for any answers was to the closest relatives of the families. In the case of the Sterlings, their closest family was a sister that lived less than ten miles from the Kurtzes' townhouse. The rest of the family lived in Alabama.

The Kurtzes, however, had plenty of family nearby. Josh Kurtz had not moved very far away from home, living within twenty miles of not only his parents, but his sister as well. And since the Miami PD had already spoken extensively with the Kurtzes earlier in the day, Mackenzie opted to check in with the sister of Julie Kurtz.

Sara Lewis seemed more than happy to meet with them, and although the news of her sister's death was less than two days old, she seemed to have accepted it as well as a twenty-two-year-old could.

Sara invited them into her house in Overtown, a quaint one-story house that was little more than a small apartment. It was decorated sparsely and held the sort of edgy silence that Mackenzie had felt in so many other houses where someone was dealing with recent loss. Sara sat on the edge of her couch, cupping a mug of tea in her hands. It was clear that she had done her fair share of crying recently; she also looked like she hadn't slept much.

"I assume that if the FBI is involved," she said, "that means there have been more murders?"

"Yes, there have," Harrison said from beside Mackenzie. She frowned briefly, wishing he had not so willingly divulged the information.

"But," Mackenzie said, interjecting before Harrison could continue, "we of course can't make any solid claims about a connection without a thorough investigation. And that's why we've been called in."

"I'll help however I can," Sara Lewis said. "But I already answered the police's questions."

"Yes, I understand, and I appreciate that," Mackenzie said. "I just want to cover a few things they might have missed. For instance, do you by any chance have any idea how your sister and brother-in-law were in terms of financial standing?"

It was clear that Sara thought it was a strange question but she did her best to answer nonetheless. "Okay, I suppose. Josh had a good job and they really didn't spend too much money. Julie would even scold me sometimes for spending too frivolously. I mean, they certainly weren't loaded...not from what I know. But they did okay."

"Now, their neighbor told us that Julie liked to draw. Was this just a hobby or was she making any money off of it?"

"More of a hobby," Julie said. "She was pretty good, but she knew it wasn't anything spectacular, you know?"

"How about ex-boyfriends? Or maybe ex-girlfriends Josh might have had?"

"Julie has a few exes, but none of them took it hard. Besides that, they all live halfway across the country. I know for a fact that two of them are married. As for Josh, I don't think there were any exes in the picture. I mean...hell, I don't know. They were just a really good couple. Really good together—disgustingly cute in public. That sort of couple."

The visit felt too brief to end but Mackenzie had only one other route to pursue and she wasn't quite sure how to refer to it without repeating herself. She thought back to those odd entries in the Sterlings' checkbook, still unable to figure them out.

Probably nothing, she thought. *People keep their checkbooks differently, that's all. Still, worth looking into.*

Thinking of the abbreviations she had seen in the Sterlings' checkbook, Mackenzie continued on. As she opened her mouth to speak, she heard Harrison's phone vibrating in his pocket. He quickly checked it and then ignored the call. "Sorry," he said.

Ignoring the disturbance, Mackenzie asked: "Would you happen to know if Julie or Josh were involved with any sort of organizations or maybe even clubs or gyms? The sort of place they'd routinely pay fees to?"

Julie thought about this for a moment but shook her head. "Not that I know of. Like I said...they didn't really spend a lot of money. The only monthly fee I know of that Julie had outside of bills was her Spotify account, and that's only ten bucks."

"And have you been contacted by anyone like an attorney about what happens with their finances?" Mackenzie asked. "I'm very sorry to ask, but it could be pressing."

"No, not yet," she said. "They were so young, I don't even know if they had drawn up a will. Shit...I guess I have all of that to look forward to, don't I?"

Mackenzie got to her feet, unable to answer the question. "Thanks again for speaking with us, Sara. Please, if you think of anything else in regards to the questions I've asked you, I'd appreciate a call."

With that, she handed Sara a business card. Sara took it and pocketed it as she led them to the door. She wasn't being rude but it was clear that she wanted them to leave as quickly as possible.

With the door closed behind them, Mackenzie found herself standing on Sara's porch with Harrison. She considered correcting him on so quickly letting Sara know that there had been more murders that could be related to the murder of her sister. But it had been an honest mistake, one that she had made once or twice when she had started off. So she let it go.

"Can I ask you something?" Harrison asked.

"Sure," Mackenzie said.

"Why were you so fixated on their finances? Did it have something to do with what you saw in the Sterlings' place?"

"Yeah. It's just a hunch for now, but some of the transactions were—"

Harrison's phone started vibrating again. He scooped it out of his pocket with an embarrassed look on his face. He checked the display, nearly ignored it, but then kept it out as they walked back toward the car.

"Sorry, I have to take this," he said. "It's my sister. She called while we were inside, too. Which is weird."

Mackenzie didn't pay him much attention as they got into the car. She was barely even listening to Harrison's end of the conversation as he started speaking. However, by the time she had pulled back out onto the street, she could tell by his tone that something was very wrong.

When he ended the call, there was a shocked expression on his face. His bottom lip had a sort of curl to it, somewhere between a grimace and a frown.

"Harrison?"

"My mom died this morning," he said.

"Oh my God," Mackenzie said.

"Heart attack…just like that. She's—"

Mackenzie could tell that he was struggling not to break down in tears. He turned his head away from her, looking out of the passenger side window, and started to let it out.

"I'm so sorry, Harrison," she said. "Let's get you back home. I'll set up the flight now. Anything else you need?"

27

He only gave a brief shake of the head, still looking away from her as he wept a bit more openly.

Mackenzie first made a call to Quantico. She was unable to get McGrath on the phone so she left a message with his receptionist, letting her know what had happened and that Harrison would be on a flight back into DC as soon as possible. She then called the airline and grabbed the first available flight, which departed in three and a half hours.

The moment the flight was booked and she ended the call, her phone rang. Giving Harrison a sympathetic look, she answered it. It felt terrible to resort back to a work mentality after Harrison's news but she had a job to do—and there were still no solid leads.

"This is Agent White," she said.

"Agent White, this is Officer Dagney. I thought you might want to know that we have a potential lead."

"Potential?" she asked.

"Well, he certainly fits the profile. This is a guy that was booked on multiple home invasions, two of which included violence and sexual assault."

"In the same areas as the Kurtzes and Sterlings?"

"That's where it gets promising," Dagney said. "One of the instances that involved sexual assault happened in the same group of townhouses the Kurtzes lived in."

"Do we have an address for the guy?"

"Yeah. He works at an auto garage. A small one. And we've got confirmation that he's there right now. Name of Mike Nell."

"Send me the address and I'll go have a talk with him. And any word on the financial records Harrison requested?" Mackenzie asked.

"Not yet. We've got some guys working on it, though. Shouldn't take too long."

Mackenzie killed the call and did her best to give Harrison his moment of grief. He was no longer weeping, but was clearly having to make an effort to keep it together.

"Thanks," Harrison said, wiping a stray tear away from his face.

"For what?" Mackenzie asked.

He shrugged. "Calling McGrath and the airport. Sorry this is such a pain in the midst of the case."

"It's not," she said. "Harrison, I'm very sorry for your loss."

After that, the car fell into silence and whether she liked it or not, Mackenzie's mind slipped back into work mode. There was a killer somewhere out there, apparently with some odd vengeance to

28

enact upon happy couples. And he might be awaiting her this very second.

Mackenzie could barely wait to meet him.

CHAPTER SEVEN

Dropping Harrison off at the motel was bittersweet. She wished she could do more for him or, at the very least, offer some more comforting words. In the end, though, she only gave him a half-hearted wave as he went into his room to pack his things and call a cab to take him to the airport.

Once his door had closed behind him, Mackenzie pasted the address Dagney had sent her into her GPS. Lipton Auto Garage was exactly seventeen minutes from the motel, a distance she started to cover right away.

Being alone in the car felt strange but she again distracted herself with the Miami scenery. It was different from any other beach-oriented city she had ever been in. Where smaller towns situated by the beach seemed a little sandy and almost faded, everything in Miami seemed to shine and sparkle despite the nearby sand and salt spray from the ocean. Here and there she would see a building that seemed out of place, neglected and forlorn—a reminder that everything had its blemishes.

She arrived at the garage sooner than she expected, having been distracted by taking in the sights of the city. She parked in a lot that was overcrowded with broken down cars and trucks that were obviously being pillaged for spare parts. It looked like the sort of operation that was forever in a state of almost going bankrupt.

Before walking into the place, she did a quick once-over of the place. There was a run-down front office that was currently unattended. The attached garage held three bays, only one of which contained a car; it was up on risers but did not look to be having any work done on it. In the garage, one man was rummaging through a shelf-shaped toolbox. Another was in the very back of the garage, standing on a small ladder and rifling through a series of old cardboard boxes.

Mackenzie walked over to the man closest to her, the one looking through the toolbox. He looked to be nearing forty, with long greasy hair that hung down to his shoulders. The stubble on his face was not quite a beard. When he looked up at her as she approached, he smiled brightly.

"Hey, darlin'," he said with a bit of a Southern accent. "What can I help you with today?"

Mackenzie flashed her badge. "You can stop calling me *darling* first of all. Then you can tell me if you happen to be Mike Nell."

30

"Yeah, that's me," he said. He was staring at her ID with something like fear. He then looked back at her face, as if trying to decide if he was part of some prank.

"Mr. Nell, I'd like for you to—"

He wheeled around quickly and shoved her. *Hard.* She stumbled backward and her feet struck a tire that was lying on the ground. As she lost her footing and went falling to her backside, she caught a glimpse of Nell running away. He was leaving the garage, running and looking over his shoulder.

That escalated quickly, she thought. *He'd sure as hell guilty of* something.

Her instincts wanted to go for her gun. But that would cause a scene. So she got up and gave chase. Yet, as she pushed herself up, her hand fell on something else that had been left on the floor. It was a lug wrench—possibly the one that had taken off the tire she had fallen over.

She picked it up and quickly got to her feet. She dashed to the front of the garage and saw Nell at the sidewalk, about to cross the street. Mackenzie quickly looked both ways, saw that there were no cars within a few feet, and drew her arm back.

She launched the lug wrench through the air with as much force as she could. It sailed over the fifteen feet or so that separated her and Nell, striking him squarely in the back. He let out a yelp of surprise and pain before staggering forward and falling to his knees, nearly face planting on the side of the street.

She ran after him, driving a knee into his back before he could even think about trying to get back to his feet.

She pinned his arms behind him and pushed down. He tried squirming but then realized that trying to get away only caused more pain as his shoulders were stretched back. With a quickness that she had been practicing for months now, she pulled the set of handcuffs from her belt and slapped them around Nell's wrist.

"That was stupid," Mackenzie said. "I only wanted to ask some questions...and you gave me the answer I was looking for."

Nell said nothing but he did finally accept that he could not get away from her. As cars passed by, the other man from the garage came rushing over.

"What the hell is this?" he asked.

"Mr. Nell just attacked an FBI agent," Mackenzie said. "I'm afraid he won't be able to finish out the day for you."

***

Mackenzie observed Mike Nell from behind the double-mirror of the observation room. He looked aggravated and embarrassed—a scowl that had remained on his face ever since Mackenzie had hauled him to his feet, handcuffed in front of his employer. He chewed nervously at his lip, an indication that he was probably itching for a cigarette or a drink.

Mackenzie looked away from him to study the file in her hands. It told the brief but troubled story of Mike Nell, a teenage runaway at the age of sixteen, busted for petty theft and aggravated assault for the first time at eighteen. The last twelve years of his life painted the portrait of a troubled loser—assault, theft, breaking and entering, a few stints in prison.

Beside Mackenzie, Dagney and Chief Rodriguez looked out at Nell with something like contempt.

"I take it you've seen a lot of him in the past?" Mackenzie asked.

"We have," Rodriguez said. "And somehow, the courts keep just slapping him on the wrist and that's it. The longest sentence he served was the one he just got paroled from, and that was for a sentence of one year. If it turns out this jackass is responsible for these murders, the courts are going to be tucking their tail between their legs."

Mackenzie handed the report to Dagney and stepped toward the door. "Well then, let's see what he has to say," she said.

She exited the room and stood in the hallway for a moment before heading in to interrogate Mike Nell. She took out her phone, looking to see if she had received a text from Harrison. She assumed he'd be at the airport by now, maybe having spoken to other family members to get a better idea of what was going on back home.. She genuinely felt sorry for him and even though she did not know him all that well, she wished there was something she could do for him.

Setting her emotions aside for the moment, she pocketed her phone and entered the interrogation room. Mike Nell looked up at her and didn't bother hiding the look of contempt. But now there was something else, too. He made no attempt to hide the fact that he was checking her out, his eyes lingering especially longer than necessary on her hips.

"See something you like, Mr. Nell?" she asked as she took a seat.

Clearly perplexed by the question, Nell chuckled nervously and said, "I guess."

"I suppose you know that you're in trouble for putting your hands on an FBI agent, even if it *was* just a push."

"What about your little lug wrench stunt?" he asked.

"Would you have preferred my gun? A shot right through the calf or shoulder to slow you down?"

Nell had nothing to say to that.

"It's clear we're not going to be best friends anytime soon," Mackenzie said, "so let's skip the small talk. I'd like to know just about everywhere you've been over the course of the last week."

"That's a long list," Nell said defiantly.

"Yes, I'm sure a man of your character gets all over the place. So let's start with two nights ago. Where were you between six p.m. and six a.m.?"

"Two nights ago? I was out with a friend. Played some cards, had a few drinks. Nothing big."

"Can anyone other than your friend vouch for that?"

Nell shrugged. "I don't know. There were a few other guys playing cards with us. What the hell is all this about anyway?"

Mackenzie didn't see the point in dragging it out any further than necessary. If she wasn't so distracted by what was going on with Harrison, she might have grilled him further before getting straight to the point, hoping he'd trip himself up if he was indeed guilty.

"A couple was found murdered in their townhouse two nights ago. It just happens to be a townhouse located in the same complex of townhouses you were busted for attempted burglary and aggravated assault. Put the two together, plus the fact that you've been paroled for a little less than a month, and that puts you high on the list of people to question."

"That's bullshit," Nell said.

"No, that's logic. Something I'm assuming you're not familiar with based on your criminal record."

She could see that he wanted to toss a remark back out to her but he stopped himself, again chewing on his bottom lip. "I haven't been back by that place since I got out," he said. "What the hell sort of sense would that make?"

She eyed him skeptically for a moment and asked: "What about your friends? Are they guys you met while in prison?"

"One of them, yeah."

"Any of your friends into burglary and assault, too?"

"No," he spat. "One of the guys has a breaking and entering charge on him from when he was a teenager, but no…they wouldn't kill anyone. Neither would I."

33

"But breaking and entering and beating someone is A-OK?"

"I never killed anyone," he said again. He was clearly frustrated and showing great restraint to not lash out at her. And that's exactly what she had been looking for. If he were guilty of the murders, the chance of him growing instantly defensive and angry would be much higher. The fact that he was doing his best to stay out of trouble, even from lashing out verbally at an FBI agent, showed that he likely had no connection to the murders.

"Okay, so let's say you're *not* connected with these murders. What *are* you guilty of? I'm assuming you're doing *something* you shouldn't. Why else would you push me, an FBI agent, and try to run?"

"I'm not talking," he said. "Not until I see a lawyer."

"Ah, I forget you're a pro at this game by now. So yeah, fine…we'll get you your lawyer. But I assume you also know how the police work. We *know* you're guilty of something. And we're going to find out what it is. So tell me now and save everyone some trouble."

His five straight seconds of silence indicated that he intended to do no such thing.

"I'm going to need the names and the numbers of the men you claim to have been with two nights ago. Give me those and if your alibi checks out, you're free to go."

"Fine," Nell grunted.

His reaction to this was yet another sign that he was likely innocent of the murders. There was no instant relief on his face, just a sort of annoyed irritation that he had somehow once again found himself back in an interrogation room.

Mackenzie took the names of the men down and noted for Dagney or whoever was in charge of such things to scroll through Nell's cell phone for their numbers. She left the interrogation room and headed back into observation.

"Well?" Rodriguez said.

"He's not our guy," Mackenzie said. "But just for protocol, here's a list of his friends he says he was with on the night the Kurtzes were murdered."

"You're sure of that?"

She nodded.

"There was no real relief when I told him he could likely leave after his alibi checked out. And I tried to get a rise out of him, to trip him up. His behavior simply is not indicative of a guilty party. But like I said, we should check the accomplices just to be sure. Nell is sure as hell guilty of something. I've got a sore backside from falling down to prove it. Think your guys can figure out what it is?"

"You got it."

She left the station, confident that Mike Nell was not their man. Somewhere beyond that, though, she started to think of her father.

She supposed it was bound to happen. There were a few similarities between his case and the current case she was on. Someone had come into the couples' homes with no signs of forced entry, insinuating that the couples knew the killer and let him in willingly. She caught flashes of her father, sprawled bloody on the bed, as she recalled the images she'd seen of the Kurtzes and Sterlings in the case files.

Thinking of a deceased parent made her feel more strongly for Harrison's situation. She got to the motel as quickly as she could, yet when she knocked on his door, he did not answer. Mackenzie walked to the front desk and found a bored-looking receptionist thumbing through a *Star* magazine.

"Excuse me, but did my partner leave?"

"Yes, he left about five minutes ago. I called him a cab to take him to the airport."

"Thank you," Mackenzie said, deflated.

She left the front office feeling strangely alienated. Sure, she'd been on a few cases alone before, especially when working as a detective in Nebraska. But being in a strange city without a partner made her feel particularly alone. It made her feel slightly uneasy but there was no use in trying to ignore it.

With that sense of displacement growing by the second, Mackenzie figured she'd put a stop to it the only way she knew how: by drowning herself in work. She got back into her car and went directly back to the station, thinking that while pursuing the case alone might be a bit depressing, it could also be just the motivation she needed to find the killer before the day came to a close.

CHAPTER EIGHT

Her motivation to bring the killer in on her own was quickly muted by a lack of answers and several hours that felt absolutely wasted back at the station. She sat in a small spare office provided by Rodriguez as the few scant updates came in. The first update was that after less than three hours, every single one of Mike Nell's accomplices had panned out. There was now evidence from multiple sources that Nell had been nowhere near the Kurtz townhouse on the night of the murders.

However, those same three hours also had Miami PD locate two pounds of heroin hiding in a small secret compartment of his truck. A few calls also proved that he had meetings to sell it, one of which was to a customer who was only fifteen years of age.

The second update was a bit more useful but really provided very little to go on. Two of the initialed entries within the Sterlings' checkbook that Mackenzie had not recognized were accounted for. One was a local animal shelter, to which they had made contributions twice a year. Another had been a small grassroots political campaign, and the other was still a mystery.

With the other two eliminated, Mackenzie was able to focus on the remaining one. The initials in question were DCM. Joey Nestler was the officer who brought her the results of the first two, and before he could leave her tiny working space, Mackenzie stopped him.

"Officer Nestler, do you have any idea what these initials might mean? Are there any businesses, organizations, or even individuals in the city that these might apply to?"

"I've been wondering that myself ever since we got the results," he said. "But I'm coming up with nothing. We've got some guys working on it, though. We're also looking over the Kurtzes' financial records to see if there's any sort of connection."

"Great work," she said.

Nestler left her alone after that. She then turned her attention back to the crime scene photos. It was weird, but the vast amount of blood in both photos was not what unsettled her the most. There was something even more gruesome about the way the bodies had been arranged. As far as she was concerned, there was no question that the bodies had been moved and staged to be lying on their backs. With the evidence of a struggle of some sort having occurred at the Sterling residence, it was all but a given that the scenes had been purposefully set up.

But why?

She kept looking at the posturing of the hands. *What's he trying to tell us? That the couples are linked somehow? Is he highlighting the couples' need for one another?*

She was fairly certain that there was some sort of symbolism in the posing of the hands in both photos: in the Kurtz photo, Julie's hand was touching her husband's thigh, almost draped lovingly over it; in the Sterling photo, it was Gerald Sterling's hand draped over his wife's thigh.

There's no way that's an accident, Mackenzie thought.

But what does it mean?

She studied each and every picture from the crime scenes but could find nothing. So rather than trying to find something new, she started to go back over things they knew for certain. By eliminating the obvious things, it at least made the list for motive a little shorter.

These murders were not just routine home invasions.

Nothing stolen. No immediate signs of forced entry.

These seemed like obvious facts but they spoke volumes. The murders were not about money, so theft could be eliminated (and was one of the main reasons Mackenzie had been so easily able to dismiss Mike Nell). And as far as she could tell they weren't blatantly about sex, either.

She kept going back to the positioning of the hands.

There has to be something to it, something there. He's killing couples and making sure their bodies touch just the slightest bit. What am I missing?

As she wracked her brain over this, a knock came to her door. She looked up and saw Rodriguez standing there.

"Hell, White…you used to working long hours?"

Mackenzie looked at her watch, shocked to see that it had somehow come to be seven in the evening. She stretched her back in the chair and closed the files in front of her.

"Yeah, time tends to sneak up on me from time to time."

"Well, I'm obviously not your boss but why not call it a day? There's really nothing much you can do here. Although we *did* just now make a possible connection. The DCM listing in the Sterlings' checkbook is probably a reference to a private club. And the thing of it is, we can't figure out what it stands for. As far as we know, there's no meaning to it—just three letters."

"What kind of club?" Mackenzie asked.

"It's a private club. But the general consensus is it's just sort of this well-to-so socialite crap. You pay a fee every so often and get to hang out with other snobby people to drink expensive wine or use a dance floor that no one else in the city can use."

"Do we have contact information?" she asked.

"Just a website that gives a phone number. But we've tried calling it and can't get an answer."

"Can you send me the link?" she asked.

"Absolutely. Now…seriously. Call it a night. We can all work together tomorrow to dig into this DCM place. The assumption is that whatever number is on the site is simply not being answered after business hours."

It sounded like a good idea. And while she'd no doubt do some investigating of her own during the night on a club named DCM, she realized that with time having slipped away from her, she was pretty hungry. Dinner, maybe a drink, and then she'd look into the website and club.

She left the station and headed back to the motel. During the drive there, the weight of being on her own on the case in an unfamiliar city once again settled on her. It wasn't just the sense of being on her own to solve a case, but being alone *period.* Something about it here, in a strange city with only people she didn't know at all to assist her, was rather sad in a way she could not describe.

Might as well play the part of the loner, she thought as she turned into the parking lot of a Papa John's. She went inside, ordered a pizza, and then walked across the parking lot to a Kroger while she waited. She picked up a six-pack of beer and a bag of chips. When she went through the self-checkout line, she felt more domesticated and depressed than she had ever since coming to Quantico.

As she walked back to pick up her pizza with her bagged six-pack of Dos Equis in hand, a comical thought crossed her mind.

I wonder what McGrath would think of me if he saw me right now. Then, on the heels of that: *If there's a Heaven and Bryers is looking down on me right now, what is* he *thinking?*

With a thin smile at that thought, she picked up her pizza and returned to the motel. She changed into comfortable clothes—a T-shirt and a pair of shorts—and opened the pizza on the table by her bed. She then opened up her laptop. She nearly started working but an idea crept into her head—a freeing idea that surprised her but was very enticing.

She placed the laptop and one of the beers on top of the pizza box, the beer lying on its glass side. She picked it all up and then left the room again but this time, she walked to the side and to a small sidewalk she had spied earlier when dropping Harrison off. She walked down this sidewalk a bit, listening to the sound of crashing waves from directly ahead. A few more feet brought her to the rear of the motel and the surrounding buildings. A wide wooden walkway separated the buildings from the beach down below.

She started out at the water as she made her way down to the sand. She kicked off her shoes and socks, carrying them awkwardly with the pizza, beer, and laptop. She loved the way the sand felt on her toes; it was nearly hypnotic, easily one of the best sensations she had felt in a very long time.

She located an empty wooden bench tucked away beside a small dune of sand and took a seat there. A few palm trees towered overhead and for the briefest of moments, she felt like she had escaped the world and was on some dreamlike vacation.

She was still about fifty yards from the ocean, but that was fine. The sound and smell of it was enough for her, as was the ocean breeze that crept up the beach. She popped open her beer, started on a slice of pizza, and then cracked open the laptop.

She typed in the link Rodriguez had texted her and was taken to a simple website. The connection was slow, as she was nearly out of the motel's Wi-Fi range, but the browser eventually took her where she needed to go. The site came up without bells and whistles. There was just a plain background with very little copy. No additional pages or dropdowns.

The copy read: *DCM. A private club. Invite only. Inquiries refer to 786.555.6869.*

It seemed pointless to even have a page if that was all the information that was going to be provided. She of course knew that with a bit of time and effort, someone with coding expertise could find out the source of the site and maybe even who owned and operated it. But she knew that there was not nearly enough suspicion about DCM just yet to warrant such a search. A few entries in the checkbook of a deceased couple could mean nothing—and probably did.

Still, the lack of any real information on the site did make her wonder. It seemed a little too suspicious for her. She nearly called up Rodriguez to see if he could get a team working on it right away but decided against it. She didn't want to come in rocking the boat, especially now that she was by herself, running the show alone.

With two slices of pizza and her first beer down, Mackenzie closed the lid of her laptop. The sky was growing dark, the ocean taking on a beautiful yet eerie quality. She was tempted to bring the rest of the beers out here, drink them by herself by the beach, and get a good buzz before retiring for the night. Yet the responsible side of her knew that it was nearly nine o'clock and she needed to get as much sleep as possible while the case had yet to pick up steam. Rotating her neck to loosen up the muscles in her shoulders, she bid the ocean a fond farewell and walked back to the motel.

Back in her room, she waited a moment to wash the sand from her feet. It was a good feeling—almost something childlike about it. After a while, though, she stripped down and allowed herself a nice, long shower.

While the hot water felt incredible and it was an overall peaceful experience, her mind would not clear. Honestly, her mind was never at rest or all clear. Even when she was relaxed and easygoing, there was always one thing remaining constant in the back of her mind: her father's case.

She'd felt for a few months now that somehow, she would be the one to close his case. Ever since it had been reopened and she had been given something of an inside peek into it, she'd felt like it was *her* case—that she should have ownership of it. And while McGrath was being lenient enough to let her have a mostly open view toward it, she understood completely why he could not assign it to her.

Besides, it looked as if there was a dead end waiting for her yet again. That damned Barker Antiques business card haunted her like a ghost from a haunted house she'd never get to visit.

She remained under the water until it started to go cold. She got out, wrapped a towel around her, and walked back out into the room, where she opened another beer. Just as she was about to swap out the towel for her night attire of a T-shirt and underwear, a knock sounded at the door.

It was such an unexpected sound that she nearly dropped her beer. Confused, she hurried to the door and looked through the peephole.

What the hell?

She looked again, just to make sure she had seen the person out there correctly.

She was so surprised that she didn't think clearly enough when she unlocked the chain and started opening the door. She did not realize that she was still in nothing but a towel until the chilled night air curled against her mostly bare and still slightly wet legs.

With the door open, there was no mistaking the identity of the person who had knocked. There was no peephole to distort their features.

She stood there, still shocked, with the door partially open.

Ellington stood on the other side with a shocked look on his face—another late reminder that she was wearing only a towel.

"What are you doing here?" she asked.

Ellington smiled at her. "Being overdressed, apparently."

CHAPTER NINE

Mackenzie allowed him inside, still not understanding what Ellington was doing there. She also had no idea why she could not unstick the logical part of her mind and rush to the bathroom to put on some damn clothes.

This man should not throw you off so badly, she thought to herself.

That was true. But she could not deny that seeing him made her feel happier than it should. She was overjoyed to see him—a joy that grew stronger than the confusion of the moment by the second.

"McGrath sent me out shortly after he received the message about Harrison's mother and his return to Quantico," Ellington explained.

"He didn't waste any time then, did he?"

"No. And before we get any further into this, I need to point out that given our past, I'd find this conversation a lot easier to have if you'd put on some clothes."

He did not say it in a mean or disrespectful way. He was being polite. More than that, she saw something else in his eyes—an almost adolescent sort of embarrassment. He *wanted* to take in what he was seeing—her body covered only from the tops of her breasts to the very tops of her thighs—but did not want to come off as being rude.

"Sorry," she said. "One second."

She retrieved her clothes from the end of the bed, adding a pair of jeans from her suitcase. She then quickly went into the bathroom. As she crossed in front of him, she saw him looking at her. It made her feel sexy, something she had not felt in quite some time.

She slipped into the bathroom, quickly closing the door behind her. She dried her hair a bit more with a towel before putting on her clothes. "There's pizza and beer," she called through the door. "Help yourself."

"Thanks," he said. "I'll take you up on the beer."

With her hair as dry as she could get it without a blow dryer, she reached for her clothes. She hesitated for a moment, looking at the door. A thought raced through her mind like a hurricane. She'd had a similar thought before and it had turned out very badly. He'd not necessarily rejected her—he had simply been trying to do the right thing.

That had been nearly two months ago, though. And with the way she had been feeling ever since Harrison left—alone, a little useless and, quite frankly *lost*—the thought felt almost justified. More than that, it felt right.

Mackenzie, what the hell are you thinking?

She sighed and set her clothes back down on the edge of the sink.

Don't do this, some small part of her screamed. *No. This could be bad. This could ruin your working relationship.*

But that was followed by another thought: *The way he looked at me a few seconds ago…there was something there.*

She reached for the doorknob with one last thought: *To hell with it.*

It had been nearly a year since she had been with a man, since she had allowed herself to be not only vulnerable with a man, but to take the time to actually enjoy not just sex, but the idea of connecting with a man over something more than work.

Mackenzie opened the bathroom door. Ellington had his back to her, looking at the case files. He had helped himself to one of the beers, taking a sip and unaware of what was standing behind him.

She felt incredibly sexy and nervous all at once. It was an intoxicating feeling.

"Okay," she said. "This better?"

He turned around and his mouth literally fell open at what he saw. He was clearly confused but he also made no attempt to look away.

"Mackenzie, what the hell are you doing?"

She stepped into the room, fully aware that she was no good at doing the sexy stuff: strutting or giving guys the come-hither stare.

"It's okay," she said. "And if you really want me to, I'll explain some stuff to you later. About my day…about the case, how I'm feeling. Or I could do it now. If you really want me to talk right now while I'm standing here like this, waiting for you, I can do that. I can—"

He put his beer down and came to her in two quick strides. He wasted no time with eye-gazing or slowly leaning in. He took her in his arms and kissed her. It was a harsh kiss but the force of it seemed to translate the tension they'd both been feeling for the better part of six months now.

Mackenzie lost herself in the kiss. It was so fast and dizzying that she wasn't fully aware that he had lowered her to the bed until she felt some of his weight on her. And after that, she lost herself again—and enjoyed every blissful second of it.

***

Afterward, they did not linger in bed, spooning or holding or staring into each other's eyes. The good thing about Ellington was that he was just as committed to work as she was. They took turns going to the bathroom to freshen up and met at the edge of the bed. Mackenzie wore the night attire she had originally intended to wear; Ellington wore only his pants, showing toned abs and shoulders that seemed just as tense now as they had been moments ago in bed.

Mackenzie sorted through the case files as Ellington started to look at them.

"And these are the only two couples so far?" he asked.

"Yes. And the only thing I have that can be considered as any sort of motive is the hands on the couples in the pictures."

"What about them?"

She pointed out how one spouse's hand had been positioned to purposefully touch their partner in each picture.

"That does seem a little strange, huh?" he said.

"It does. The question is whether it's just some strange sort of calling card for the killer or if it means the killer believes the two couples are somehow linked."

"Do you think such a clue means that maybe these two are the only victims?"

"I don't know," Mackenzie answered. "With two couples involved, it's difficult to tell. If it were just one couple, I'd be looking for a jilted lover or a jealous ex. I've asked about such things from the family of Julie Kurtz and it's not looking like an option anyway."

"Have you had *any* breaks?"

"Not really," she said. She cracked her laptop back open and showed him the DCM website. "This is the only thing of interest. DCM was a listing in the Sterlings' checkbook. And we're still not even one hundred percent sure their DCM is this place."

"Still, an exclusive club with a shady website…that's always worth looking into," Ellington pointed out.

"My thoughts exactly."

Ellington thought things over for a bit and then said: "I don't want to come in and assume that this is my case as much as it is yours. You're leading this thing. McGrath just sent me out to help."

"You didn't request it?"

"No. He knows we work well together. It was a smart move on his part. I think he regrets lining you up with Harrison. We're a better fit for the job, I think."

44

They both let the weight of that comment sink in. The case files sat in front of them and the reality of what they had just done hung in the air. It wasn't tense but it also seemed to carry a tinge of uneasiness.

"Okay, I'll be the sleazy guy and drop some innuendo," Ellington said. "Should I go ahead and get my own room for the night?"

Mackenzie considered this for a while before finally nodding. "Yes. I think you should. If for nothing else than to eliminate suspicion when the expense reports are submitted."

"Good thinking," he said. "I'll go get my own room. But afterwards, I was thinking I might come back here and instigate some things."

"While I do think you need your own room," Mackenzie said, "I see no need to wait for the instigating."

She smiled at him and stretched out on the bed.

"If the invitation looks like that, what I'd be doing would not be instigating," he said. "White, it's all in the details."

"Oh my God," she scoffed. "Would you shut up and just get over here?"

With a smile of his own, Ellington obliged.

CHAPTER TEN

Mackenzie made her way slowly through the house she grew up in. Her mother was asleep on the couch. She stopped and looked at her. It was her mother as she preferred to remember her, back when she still had some of her looks and probably even clung to a few of the dreams for her life that would ultimately never come true.

She ran a hand softly over her mother's face. She left a thin trail of wet blood.

She made her way through the small living room, down the hallway and toward her parents' bedroom. She slowly opened the door and saw her father. He was sleeping, one leg kicked out from under the covers. He did not stir as she entered the room. He was deeply asleep.

She lifted her hand and saw that she was carrying a gun—a basic pistol of some kind, the make and model of which she could not determine in the dream.

She tiptoed to her father, placed the gun to his head.

She pulled the trigger.

Mackenzie awoke at 5:22, breathing hard.

She rolled over and groaned, and willed herself to go back to sleep, to push it from her head.

She managed to barely drift off again for a bit. The next time she was stirred awake, it was by the alarm on her phone at 6:15. Beside her, the bed was empty.

It was a decision they had come to shortly before midnight. While they didn't regret the sex (yet), they realized that there was something a little more intimate about sleeping in the same bed. It was an amicable decision and as she got out of bed, Mackenzie was refreshed and surprised to see that she had zero regrets about her actions last night.

She showered again, having worked up a bit of a sweat last night. A small part of her was a bit ashamed of how brazen she had been. While she'd had two one-night stands in college, they had been the result of too much drinking and a need to be rebellious. She had never done something as blatant as she had last night…and something about it felt almost revolutionary. It was more than simple growth—it was confidence. And that confidence had very little to do with her appearance. It was more about how she felt about herself…a sense of control and self-reliance that she was only now starting to understand.

When she stepped out of the shower, she heard her phone ringing from the other room. For the second time in less than twelve hours, she found herself rushing out of the bathroom wrapped only in a towel. On the display of her phone, she saw an unfamiliar number with a Miami area code.

"This is Agent White," she answered.

"Agent White, this is Joey Nestler. The chief wanted me to call you."

"Is everything okay?"

"No," Nestler said. "We've found another murdered couple."

Her heart skipped a beat in dread.

"Text me the address," she said.

Mackenzie hung up and got dressed quickly. As she closed the door behind her, she saw Ellington coming back from the front office carrying two cups of coffee. He was dressed for the day and looked content. She wondered how he was feeling about last night but shut such thoughts down quickly. She could not let last night's fling get in the way of the case.

"Glad to see you're up and at 'em," Mackenzie said. "I just got a call from one of the officers involved with the case. They found another murdered couple."

The good mood that had been painted on his face drooped a bit. He nodded and offered her one of the coffees, which she took graciously.

"Well then, let's get to work," he said.

And just like that, they were working together again. And she realized that Ellington had been right about last night. Something about it felt natural. They were indeed a good fit...now, apparently, in more ways than one.

***

The third couple lived not too far away from the Kurtzes' townhouse. It was a modest little house tucked away behind a well-to-do subdivision, owned by Stephen and Toni Carlson. Palm trees lined the streets in a generic sort of way. The lawns were beautiful and evenly mowed, perfectly symmetrical as were the edging and flowerbeds. Inside the couple's house, though, things weren't quite so idyllic.

Mackenzie entered with Ellington, Rodriguez, and Nestler. The front door opened onto a spacious living room that wasn't really messy, but was in need of a clean. Books were scattered here and there, a stray plate remained on the coffee table, and two blankets were balled into messy piles on the couch.

As Mackenzie studied the condition of the living room, the smell hit her for the first time.

She'd smelled it only once before but knew quite well what it was.

It was the smell of something dead. Something that had been dead for quite some time.

"Jesus," Rodriguez said, angling to the front of the room.

"The officer on duty said the master bedroom is in the back," Nestler said. "He warned us that it was pretty fucking gruesome. Dispatch said he was damn near in tears."

"How did he learn about the bodies in the first place?" Mackenzie asked, lowering her head in an attempt to cut down on the stench.

"The husband's boss called the police yesterday after he was unable to get him on the phone or via text or email over the last five days."

"His boss?" Ellington asked. "That seems weird."

"He was apparently a workaholic," Nestler explained. "He was in charge of business development with this military-funded telecommunications company. For him to miss *one* day without calling in beforehand was weird enough. After the fifth day with no word at all, the boss got worried. Even drove over here last night and knocked on the door but no one answered. He saw both cars in the driveway and placed the call."

That was all Mackenzie needed to hear. Still holding her head down against the smell, she forged on. She also noticed that the house was quite humid, which obviously did nothing to help the smell. She spied the thermostat on the living room wall and saw that it was currently eighty-two degrees inside. She placed the air down to seventy degrees and heard the air conditioning kick on elsewhere in the house.

They exited the living room, walking through a large kitchen and then into the only hallway in the house. As they passed through the kitchen, the smell intensified. Behind her, Nestler coughed and let out a little moan.

As they made their way down the hall toward the bedroom, Rodriguez stepped aside for a moment to allow Mackenzie and Ellington to go ahead of him. As she approached the door the smell was worse than ever and it was then that she noticed just how stuffy and stagnant the house felt. It felt like walking in a tomb.

The bedroom door was closed. Mackenzie pushed it slowly open and the first thing she saw were the maroon streaks on the walls.

Then, of course, there was the murdered couple in the bed—the Carlsons.

Like the previous couples, they were lying on their backs. They had been borderline butchered, with several large gashes in their stomachs and chests. Stephen Carlson had also had his throat slashed. Toni Carlson was wearing a silk nightie, soaked in blood. Stephen wore a pair of boxers.

The blood was dried, congealed in some places. It was all over the carpet on Toni's side of the room. The definite shape of a footprint could be seen.

"A potential struggle," Mackenzie said, pointing to the area.

She got nods in response. It seemed like everyone was afraid to speak, not wanting to take in the stench of the place any more than was absolutely necessary.

The smell was thick here, almost like another wall within the room. Rigor mortis had most definitely set in. The skin on both of them was pale, nearly white in some areas.

"I think it's safe to say the Carlsons were killed before the Sterlings or Kurtzes," Rodriguez said in a thin and choked voice.

"But not too long beforehand," Mackenzie said. "Maybe by two days. Three at most. That means that this guy has killed six people in the span of six or seven days."

Willing herself forward, Mackenzie walked closer to the bed. She eyed the cuts and gashes. It was quite clear that a knife had been used. But this realization was almost secondary. What her eyes were focused on was Toni Carlson's left hand. It was resting on her husband's thigh.

Just like the other two crime scenes.

"What the hell is going on?" Rodriguez asked. "This can't just be home invasion shit, right?"

"Definitely not," Mackenzie said. "I'm betting this is just like the other cases. We'll have a look around the house and I guarantee you there will be no signs of forced entry. Just like the Kurtzes and Sterlings, I bet the killer just walked right in. Probably invited."

"Nestler, can you start looking for signs of a break-in?" Rodriguez asked.

"Gladly," Nestler said, making his way quickly out of the room.

Mackenzie turned away from the bed. She glanced around the room, very tidy with the exception of the blood on the walls and carpet. She checked Stephen's bedside table. There were a pair of reading glasses and a biography on John Kennedy. Toni's held a glass of water and a tacky romance novel.

She then made her way into their closet. Like the bedroom it was mess-free. Stephen's clothes were hung on the right wall, Toni's on the left. A shelf along the back wall held a few decorative bags. A small handheld video camera sat among the bags. On a shelf beneath the bags were about a dozen small cartridge-like cassettes. Upon closer inspection, Mackenzie saw that these were mini-tapes…likely created with the handheld recorder. On the front label of each tape was a date. Some dated back as far as seven years. The most recent was from two years ago.

Tapes located in a bedroom closet, she thought. *Pretty sure what that means. Might be worth looking into for clues, though.*

To test her theory, she unzipped one of the bags and peered inside. She saw handcuffs lined with velvet, various sex toys, and a few blindfolds.

Yeah…I was right.

A little embarrassed, she zipped the bag back up and walked back out into the room. "There are a few videos in there," she said. "Pretty sure they're homemade sex movies. They might warrant a look. If they willingly invited someone in and they were as sexually adventurous as their closet indicates, there could be a link there."

"I'll get someone on it," Rodriguez said.

Mackenzie stood at the end of the bed again, looking for something she might have missed here or at the other scenes. But there was nothing. Just a world of red and the overwhelming stench of death.

She exited the room with Ellington behind her. Rodriguez came out third and they walked to the next doorway down the hall. It was a small study of sorts, a room split between an office and a makeshift library. A single desk sat against the near wall while four bookshelves lined the back wall.

Mackenzie glanced at some of the titles along the shelves, getting a further peek into the life of the Carlsons. *Erotica in the 1500s, Sex and Enlightenment, Tantric Secrets, Sexual Exploration in Marriage.*

On one of the shelves, she saw a small box. She recognized it right away as the sort of box that business cards came in. She looked inside and saw roughly one hundred business cards, all adorned with Stephen Carlson's name and the contact information for what she assumed was a home-based business called *Carlson Accounting.*

50

She thumbed through them and saw that the stack differed in the back. The last nine business cards were for other businesses—ones Stephen Carlson had apparently collected over the years. There was one for a plumber, one for a party planner, two different cards for auto shops in the area, one for an accountant...and then one that made Mackenzie stop.

"Ellington, look at this," she said, plucking one of the last cards out of the box.

He came over and they looked at it together.

DCM. Invite Only. There was an address and then, beneath that, *Gloria: 786-555-0951.*

"That's a different number than what we saw on the site, isn't it?" Ellington asked.

"Yes, it is. And it's also our first real lead."

CHAPTER ELEVEN

When Gloria Benitez answered Mackenzie's call, she sounded cheerful and very pleasant. She had a voice fit for marketing, particularly cold calls.

"Hello?" Gloria said.

"Ms. Benitez, this is Agent Mackenzie White with the FBI. I was hoping to have a word with you."

There was a pause before Gloria responded. When she finally did reply, most of the cheer was gone from her voice. "Can I ask what this is in regards to?"

"There has been a string of murders over the course of the last week. Three couples, to be exact. We believe at least two of them are connected to a club known as DCM. One of the couples had a business card with your number on it. And do far, you're the only link between the victims."

"My God," she said. "Who…can I ask *who*?"

Mackenzie considered it for a moment and decided to tell her. If nothing else, it would give her time to look through her records between now and whenever they met.

"The Kurtzes, the Sterlings, and the Carlsons."

The silence from the other end of the line was thick. She could hear Gloria breathing and when she finally spoke again, her voice was thin and fragile. It was hard to tell over the phone but Mackenzie thought Gloria's shock and sadness were genuine.

"What can I do for you, Agent White?"

"I'd like to meet with you as soon as possible to ask some questions about these couples. I have the address of DCM. Are you there now?"

"No, but I can be in ten minutes."

Mackenzie was pleased with the rapid response and, as such, found herself parking the car in front of a very plain yet well-maintained building in Midtown less than an hour after leaving the Carlson residence. It was the sort of building that managed to hide itself in the size and glamour of most of the surrounding buildings. The building had no sign to promote a business, not even in vinyl letters on the door.

What Mackenzie *did* see in the door was a woman standing on the other side, waiting for them. She was quite svelte, wearing a pair of too-tight yoga pants and a shirt that stopped far above her navel. She had shining blonde hair and a look that Mackenzie was quite sure had ensnared more than a few men.

As soon as Mackenzie parked the car, Gloria stepped out of the building to meet them on the sidewalk. She looked up and down the street, as if making sure no one was spying on what was happening. While there was some foot traffic on the streets, no one that passed seemed to notice or care about what was occurring between the three people in front of the nondescript building.

A quick round of introductions were made before Gloria led them into the building. When Mackenzie and Ellington were inside, Gloria locked the door behind them. As she led them down a small corridor, Gloria turned her head so that she could speak to them. She seemed like a very reluctant tour guide.

"This building is more or less DCM headquarters," she said with a little smirk. "If DCM were a country club, this building would be the clubhouse."

The corridor came to an end, opening up into a small yet elegant room. A bar area sat to the left, all the glasses turned up and the space behind the bar empty. A few booths sat along the other wall with four bar-style tables between the booths and the bar.

"And what sort of club *is* DCM?" Mackenzie asked.

"We're a club for swingers," she said.

Mackenzie rarely found herself shocked but was taken aback at this comment. *Whoa,* she thought. *Didn't see that one coming. This opens up a ton of possibilities for the case.*

"As in spouse-swapping?" Ellington asked, clearly as startled by the revelation as Mackenzie was.

"That's a more crude way to put it," Gloria said, "but yes."

"And it's by invitation only, correct?" Mackenzie asked.

"Yes," Gloria confirmed. "More often than not, new couples are referred by existing members."

"And this building is what, exactly?" Mackenzie asked.

"It's mostly a meeting spot. If two or more couples get connected and want to learn more about one another before becoming intimate, they use this building. We also often have meet-and-greet type events here once a month or so."

"And how many couples are currently members?" Mackenzie asked.

"Currently, I believe we have forty-one couples. Well…after what you told me on the phone, I suppose it's thirty-eight now."

"So you *can* confirm that all three couples were members?"

"Yes."

"Gloria, do you allow singles to take part in what goes on here?" Mackenzie asked.

"We do, but the pool is selective. Again, it's all by referrals. Sometimes a couple doesn't want to swing with another couple…they just want one more individual in the mix. And if they don't have willing friends, we'll take care of that part for them."

"Are you basically the owner?" Mackenzie asked.

"My husband and I started the club, yes. He passed away two years ago, though. And I know it may sound morbid, but I felt I needed to keep this place open. I know swinging has a sort of negative stereotype but when you see the results from my end of things, you know the real story."

"What *is* the real story?" Mackenzie asked.

Gloria thought about it for a while and when she answered, she seemed to be genuine and sincere. "Some couples that come in just really enjoy sex. And they are comfortable enough with their marriage to experiment with things like this. Some find out quickly that it is not for them and leave. Others, however, find that it enhances their sex lives and stay with us.

"There are others that come here because marriage has killed their sex drive. We're talking people that have been married for twenty years or more. They want a spark. Their marriages are dry and boring. Then they join DCM. I've seen marriages turned around from what we do here."

Personally, Mackenzie found this hard to believe. She'd always viewed swinging or any of its offsets as a form of adultery. And no matter how cool or laid back a spouse was, there was always going to be an aspect of jealousy involved.

Jealousy is probably the driving motive behind these murders, Mackenzie thought. *That, or some sort of rejection. And it gives us a motive—a reason for someone to target couples.*

"Did you know any of the murdered couples well?" Mackenzie asked.

"Honestly, I only had an actual working relationship with the Sterlings," Gloria said. "I'd hooked them up with other couples a few times. I knew the Carlsons only by name. Toni was a very beautiful woman so her name came up quite a lot in conversations. As for the Kurtzes, I met them once a few years ago. I'm pretty sure they hadn't had any DCM activity in over a year. Maybe more."

"And can you think of any links between them?" Ellington asked.

"Not right off the top of my head, no."

"Did one of the couples perhaps refer the others to DCM?"

Gloria started to look very uncomfortable. She looked at the floor for a moment, clearly wrestling with something. "Look," she finally said. "In an industry like this, I have to protect the privacy of my clients and members. Surely you can understand that. And if we get much deeper into this line of questioning, I'm going to be betraying that."

"And what about a list of couples that these three murdered couples were involved with?"

"I don't know…it just seems wrong. A betrayal of trust."

Mackenzie knew that she was right but was hoping the fact that three of her member couples had recently died might make her lose sight of it.

"Have you ever had any members you had to kick out of DCM for any reason?" Mackenzie asked.

"Only two. One was simply a financial issue. The other…well, the couple was just too much trouble. The husband was violent and borderline abusive and the wife had this weird dominatrix thing going—and not in a sexy way, either. In a lewd and almost gratuitously horrific way."

"Did any of the three murdered couples have relations with this couple?"

Again, Gloria looked to the floor. "Shit," she said. "Fine…look, I'll give you this much. But that's it. And even with this, I'd appreciate you not letting anyone know where you got the information. DCM is already scrutinized enough as it is."

"I understand," Mackenzie said. "Please. What can you tell me?"

"The couple we had to kick out was Jack and Vanessa Springs. They seemed perfect at first. Good-looking, moderately wealthy, and everyone seemed to get along with them. But when couples engaged with them, it was a different story. The incident we kicked them out for involved a couple that was *not* one of these poor murdered couples. They went back to that couple's house and at some point, the wife of the other couple knew things were getting out of hand. It got bad. The husbands got into a fight that turned rather bloody. Vanessa Springs apparently abused the other wife with some sort of sex toy. And when word got out about it, I started to get whispers from other couples that had engaged with them reporting similar activity. One of those couples was the Kurtzes."

"Do you know how often the Kurtzes and the Springs got together?"

"No. But I'm pretty sure it was at least three times."

"Forgive me," Ellington said, "but I have to ask. What other rooms are here in this building? Do people ever hook up here?"

"From time to time, yes they do. But there's no money exchanging hands."

"Then what's the fee for the club for?" Mackenzie asked.

"People pay DCM a membership fee for my services only. And by *services* I mean keep them in the network of couples and play matchmaker."

"And do you ever participate with any of your members?" Mackenzie asked.

Gloria gave her a hurt yet almost angry look. "I'm not answering that question," she said. "That has nothing to do with your investigation."

So that's a yes.

"So what *can* you tell me about the investigation, then?" Mackenzie asked. "The one link we have between these three couples is DCM. And we didn't even know the Kurtzes were members until you confirmed it on the phone."

"Well, when couples apply for membership, we do check to see if there is any history of violence or any other red flags. That's one of the reasons I was so shocked when the Springses ended up being a problem. Nothing came up in their background checks. So what I'm saying is that I find it very hard to believe that I have a member that is murdering people."

"Well, you just said yourself that the Springs couple surprised you," Ellington pointed out.

"Yes, they did. Still…there has to be some other option."

"And there might be," Mackenzie said. "One very possible option is that there is someone that may know about DCM and disapproves of it. Maybe someone jilted—like someone that applied but didn't make the cut."

"That would actually be a short list," Gloria said.

"Then it wouldn't be a problem getting it together for us?" Mackenzie asked.

This seemed like a good avenue to pursue. *These could be strange revenge killings of a sort from an embarrassed or rejected member of the club,* she thought.

Gloria again looked at odds with her situation but she eventually nodded. "Yes. I can get that together for you. I'll also get you the list of couples that are linked to the three deceased couples. I can't imagine it's long, though."

"And the contact information for the Springses, too, please," Mackenzie added.

Gloria gave a nod and turned away from them. She headed to the back of the room and walked through a door, headed elsewhere within the building.

"So this took a weird turn, huh?" Ellington said.

"That's putting it mildly," Mackenzie said.

"Lots of weird turns in the last day or so," Ellington added with a smile.

"If you're referring to last night and calling it weird, I'm not quite sure how to respond to that."

"Well, it was a *good* weird. A weird I'd like to revisit to maybe come up with a better term."

While the back-and-forth was enjoyable, she knew that she could not let her mind get sidetracked. She swerved her mind back on track, fully aware that with a link between three dead couples and a solid lead, the case might be over faster than she had dared hope.

And then perhaps she and Ellington could be *weird* again sooner rather than later.

It was a lame source of motivation, but she was rather ashamed to find that it worked. As they waited for Gloria to return with the information, Mackenzie thought back to those three dead couples, particularly the butchered state the Carlsons had been in.

All that blood. That stench.

And just like that, her mind was nowhere near thoughts of another romp between the sheets with Ellington. Instead, they were focused on finding a killer that, if her hunch was right, had stood in the very room she was currently in at some point in the past.

CHAPTER TWELVE

A series of phone calls all led Mackenzie to the obvious conclusion that both Jack and Vanessa Springs worked rigorous jobs. Any attempt to get either of them on the phone was fruitless. It was so frustrating that Mackenzie nearly decided to visit their places of employment with no regard for their reputations. In the end, though, common sense prevailed. She and Ellington spent a few hours of the afternoon in the precinct, going over the finer details of DCM and Gloria Benitez with Rodriguez and his crew. A request was made to come up with a list of criminals with sexual deviancy of any kind on their records, which Dagney started on right away.

As the afternoon wound down, Mackenzie and Ellington headed back out near Midtown. As it turned out, the Springses lived only fifteen minutes away from DCM headquarters. They lived in a trendy subdivision where there was a pool in nearly every backyard—yards that looked like someone had copied and pasted images from travel brochures and plopped them down behind each residence.

When Mackenzie parked in the driveway, she saw no cars. That maybe meant nothing, though, as both doors to the massive garage were closed.

"If they still aren't home," Ellington said, "I say we go for a dip in the pool. Do you see the size of this thing?"

Mackenzie cast a look toward the pool, surrounded by an elaborate wooden fence, and shook her head. The pool itself probably cost more than any house she'd ever dreamed of owning. And while the Springses' residence didn't look massive from the outside, it had the look of a place that had tons of treasures and secrets inside.

They walked up a series of polished concrete stairs to the front door. Mackenzie rang the bell and thought it was a little peculiar that a club such as DCM could attract such a wide range of people—from the Springses with their home that was easily worth more than a million dollars, to the Kurtzes in their simple little townhouse. She wondered how much the fee was for membership with DCM.

After thirty seconds or so, the door was answered by a woman in a very revealing bikini. It was the second time of the day where Mackenzie found herself at a momentary loss for words. The woman standing in front of them, blocking the open door, was a clichéd big-breasted blonde. Mackenzie was pretty sure she wasn't wearing any makeup, nor did she need to. She looked to be around thirty-five or so but had the complexion of a sixteen-year-old.

"Yes?" the woman said, grinning almost maliciously as she noticed how startled both Mackenzie and Ellington were.

"Hi," Mackenzie got out. "Are you Vanessa Springs?"

"I am," she said. "And you are?"

"We're Agents White and Ellington with the FBI."

"Oh?" The confidence she'd shown since coming to the door faltered a bit and Mackenzie took far too much joy from it. "FBI? What can I help with?"

"Is your husband, Jack, home?" she asked.

"Yes. We were just finishing up a swim. I think he's changing right now, actually."

"Can we come in?" Mackenzie asked. "We need to ask you some questions concerning a couple you may know—Josh and Julie Kurtz."

Vanessa thought about the name for about two seconds before recognition came over her face. And it was not a smile or beaming *a-ha* look.

Another voice came from the house behind them.

"Wait a damn minute…who is this?"

A man stepped into view. He was wearing a pair of short swimming trunks that weren't quite Speedos. Like Vanessa, he had a toned and chiseled body.

"Jack Springs?" Mackenzie asked.

"Yeah. Who the hell are you?"

Before Mackenzie could answer, Vanessa cut in. "They're with the FBI. They want to know about the Kurtzes."

"Yeah, I heard that part," Jack Springs said. "And that's why I'm going to ask you to kindly get the hell off of our property."

"I'm afraid I can't do that," Mackenzie said.

"Look," Jack said. "I don't know what those assholes have told you, but I'm getting sick of having my name dragged through the mud and I—"

"They've said nothing about you," Mackenzie said, interrupting in a loud voice. "They've been murdered. Along with two other couples. And they were all members of DCM—a club I believe you two were once affiliated with."

She clearly saw the shock on both their faces when she mentioned that the Kurtzes had been killed. What she did not see, though, was remorse. In fact, she was pretty sure she saw something very much like relief on the face of Jack Springs.

"Sorry to hear that," Jack said. "But I'm done talking about them."

With that, he tried to close the door. Ellington stepped up and held a hand out, preventing the door from closing.

"Here's the thing," Ellington said. "You either cooperate and give us a few minutes of your time, or you can force us to get a warrant to search your house."

"For what, exactly?" Vanessa asked.

"Anything regarding the Kurtzes."

"But we don't have anything—"

"Oh, and let me add," Mackenzie interrupted, "that if we are clumsy with the channels we go through in getting the warrant, the media won't have much of a problem discovering that you've had FBI agents looking around in your home."

Jack started to tremble. Mackenzie recalled the violent streak Gloria said he'd had. She tensed up, ready for anything.

"Your call, genius," Ellington said.

And that was all it took. Jack Springs took one huge stride forward and shoved Ellington. It was a rather hard shove but Ellington managed to keep his footing, only stumbling back the slightest bit.

"I'm so glad you did that," Ellington said with a sly smile. "That's technically assault on a federal agent." He withdrew his cuffs and showed them to Jack. "Can I just put these on you now, or do you want to make a spectacle out of it?"

Mackenzie could see in Jack's face that he realized he'd made an enormous mistake. He sighed and shook his head angrily.

"Good choice," Ellington said, stepping forward and slapping the cuffs on Jack's thick wrists.

CHAPTER THIRTEEN

Mackenzie made sure that Vanessa and Jack Springs were separated as soon as they got to the precinct. Once the initial juvenile reaction of most of the male officers over Vanessa Springs passed, the Springses were quickly ushered into separate rooms. Because Jack had been the one under arrest, he was placed in an interrogation room, where Ellington and Rodriguez questioned him.

Mackenzie, meanwhile, took Vanessa Springs to the tiny office she had been borrowing since arriving in Miami yesterday. She offered Vanessa a coffee and a creaking rollaway chair that had been collecting dust in the corner, and then sat down face-to-face with her.

"I'm going to assume you know why we separated you and your husband," Mackenzie said.

"So we'd answer the same questions and you could compare our answers to see if we're lying or not," Vanessa said. She was trying her best to seem defiant but it was clear that she was frightened and out of her element.

"That's right," Mackenzie said. "So the best thing to do is to tell the truth. And whether you realize it or not, your husband's reaction to the mere name of the Kurtzes tells me enough to know that there's *something* worth looking into."

Vanessa took a moment to compose herself, biting at her lip and blinking rapidly in order to stave off tears. "He's so damned stupid," she said. "Whenever he's questioned or threatened in any way, he loses his temper. He's like a little boy."

"Okay, so let's take him out of the equation for right now," Mackenzie said. She knew that Vanessa's disappointment in her husband might make this conversation much easier. "Tell me about the Kurtzes. Did you first meet them through DCM?"

"You know," she said, a little embarrassed, "no one is supposed to know who is a member. The privacy aspect was one of the reasons we decided to join."

"I know. But we spoke to Gloria Benitez this morning. When she heard that there were three murdered couples, she was very helpful. She only gave us names, though. She did not go into detail. And it tore her up to give us the information she *did* give us."

Vanessa nodded and said, "Yes, we met them through DCM."

"Did they approach you or did you approach them?"

"We told Gloria what we wanted...the sort of couple we were looking for. She hooked us up with them."

"Do you know why?"

Vanessa looked at the floor, clearly starting to get embarrassed. "We asked for a couple that was attractive and of modest means. The wife…she was gorgeous. But she was also petite. And I…that appealed to me. I like to be in control in the bedroom. And Jack doesn't. So we thought a smaller pretty woman would…I don't know. Spice things up."

"And what about Josh Kurtz?"

"We didn't even want him. But they were a couple deal. He came as part of the package, you know? And when they got to our house and we were in the bedroom, he got adventurous. He started messing with me and I let him. Part of the game and all. It was nice, I guess. But Jack wasn't prepared for seeing it. He got mad. And…ah shit. I'm ashamed of all of this…"

"It's okay," Mackenzie said. "You can skip the gory details. I just need to know of any altercations."

"Well, they started fighting and…well, it turned me on. So I sort of pinned Julie down. I thought she liked it. She didn't fight much. But I got carried away…fed on by the way Jack was behaving…"

"Did anyone get hurt?" Mackenzie asked.

"No, not really. There was one punch thrown and then they just sort of wrestled. Once Jack let Josh go, the Kurtzes left. They lodged a complaint with DCM and Gloria kicked us out."

"Was that the first couple you guys had ever contacted through DCM?"

"No. There were two others. But both of those times went smoothly."

"I guess I still don't understand why Jack got so upset about mentioning them," Mackenzie said. "He acted like there was some great drama with them."

"There was afterwards," she said. "Jack wouldn't shut up about Julie. He was infatuated with her and had no problem letting me know it. It became such an issue that we considered the idea of an open marriage. But in the end we decided against it. So you take the fact that some marriage troubles stemmed from the Kurtzes and then the fact that they ratted Jack out to Gloria, and then throw Jack's sordid temper into it all…"

"He took it personally," Mackenzie said.

"Yeah, basically."

Mackenzie thought about this for a moment before going on.

Based on this, Jack Springs is certainly worthy of closer speculation, she thought. *But I wonder if he could kill these people without Vanessa knowing.*

She wondered how Ellington was doing with his questioning of Jack.

"Vanessa, what was your impression of the Kurtzes before things got out of hand?"

"They were really sweet," she said. "They were one of those couples that are sickeningly happy when they were with one another. You could tell they really loved each other. We had dinner before we went to the bedroom. I was sort of shocked that they were involved in swingers' clubs. But Jack and I are a perfect example of the whole *different strokes for different folks* thing, you know?"

"You said the Kurtzes were involved in swingers' *clubs*?" Mackenzie asked. "As in more than one?"

"Yeah. They mentioned this other one they used to be a part of before DCM. I think it was a little sketchy for them, though."

"Do you remember the name of it?"

"Tidal Hills," Vanessa said with a low tone to her voice. "Jack and I had heard of it before, and never in a good light."

"Is that here in Miami?"

"Yeah. It's on some piece of private land out near Biscayne Bay. It markets itself very quietly as a spiritual retreat. But everyone in the swinging community knows what it really is."

"And it has a bad reputation?" Mackenzie asked.

"Yeah. Basically anyone can get in. And at the risk of sounding snobby, there's slim pickings. With DCM, it's more private so you know the people are well groomed, respectable, and good-looking."

Honey, that goes way beyond snobby...especially for a woman like you that has obviously had a major boob job.

"Have you and Jack ever participated with another swinging club?"

"There are sporadic events here and there," she said. "We've gone to a few of those. We leave for one tomorrow, actually. It's a private cruise. But no, no other clubs."

"Was there anything else about the Kurtzes you think I should know?"

"Nothing I can think of."

"What about the Sterlings and Carlsons? Did you know them?"

"No. I do remember almost inquiring about the Sterlings, though. They seemed very interesting to us. But in the end, we went with the Kurtzes."

Mackenzie was nearing the end of her questions, which was just as well. A knock on her makeshift office's door broke her attention. She turned and saw Ellington standing there. He looked relieved and satisfied.

"You good here?" he asked. "Need anything?"

Mackenzie looked at Vanessa and nodded. "Anything you want to add?"

Vanessa shook her head. "Sorry Jack came after you," she said, looking at Ellington. "Like I was telling your partner here...he can be a dick sometimes."

"No worries," Ellington said. "He was cooperative, believe it or not. He's filling out some forms right now, but you're free to go as soon as he's done."

Vanessa Springs gave them a polite little nod and then left the office. Dagney stepped in behind Ellington and led Vanessa to the front of the building. When they were gone, Ellington stepped into the small office and looked around.

"Nice digs," he said.

"Funny. What did you get out of the charming Mr. Springs?"

"Other than jealousy and the feeling that I need to up my workout routine? A decent bit. He admitted to getting violent with Josh Kurtz when the couples were together. He also admitted to once having a slight obsession with Julie Kurtz. But other than that, nothing. He gave alibis for the suspected dates of the murders and they all checked out."

"Sounds like they were telling the same story, then," Mackenzie said.

"I also think I know another spot for us to check for leads," Ellington said.

"Might it happen to be out on Biscayne Bay?"

"It would."

Mackenzie checked her watch. "It's barely seven," she said. "Want to ride out that way to see what we can find?"

"Sounds like a plan. And if we can grab some dinner along the way, maybe we can even call it a date."

She grinned at him as she got up. "We're not dating," she said. "We're only sleeping together."

"Ah, then it seems like we're on just the right case."

She cringed as they headed out of the office. "That's in terrible taste, Ellington."

He shrugged and when she passed by him, she ignored the fierce desire that passed through her, begging her to kiss him.

She considered it a victory that she was able to fight the urge off. Now that they were getting leads and she was feeling active and productive, the case was at the forefront of her mind.

They had momentum on her side now. And as far as she was concerned, the thrill of an unfolding case was an even better sensation than great sex.

CHAPTER FOURTEEN

The closer they got to Biscayne Bay, the more of the Miami skyline Mackenzie was able to see. Better yet, Ellington had volunteered to drive, allowing her to not only eat her drive-thru cheeseburger and fries unhindered, but to marvel at the looming sunset over Miami.

"Sort of weird, isn't it?" Ellington said. "You always hear about things like swingers' clubs but always assume they're just this underground thing. But now, just a few hours into this, it's just another day."

"You're not being affected by the seedy underbelly of an otherwise beautiful city, are you?"

"Beautiful?" Ellington said. "Hardly. This is the home of the Dolphins."

"A sports reference? Really?"

He shrugged. "I've got to keep you thinking about how macho I am if I plan to get you back into bed."

She rolled her eyes at him, but the idea of being back in bed with him had kept popping up in her head all day, too. It was essentially a late-twenties version of crushing on someone in middle school. It made her uneasy but, at the same time, it excited her. It was just a shame that they had finally crossed this line while she was in the middle of a particularly gruesome case.

They arrived at Biscayne Bay just as the setting sun started to cast golden hues on the tops of the buildings and the caps of the waves pulsing in the sea. From the edge of the bay, it was incredibly beautiful.

They arrived at the entrance of Tidal Hills several minutes later. The sign in front of the entrance didn't even have the name of the place on it. All the sign said was: *A private resort.*

"Looks appropriately shady," Mackenzie said.

Ellington drove closer to the building, up a small road that emptied into a parking lot that was hidden by a grove of palm trees and a small privacy fence. When he parked, Mackenzie noticed that from behind the palms and the privacy fence, the main road that coasted along the bay could not be seen.

There were a few other cars in the lot, but no person in sight. They got out of the car together and walked to the building behind them. The place was built to resemble a beach house, highlighted along the porch with weathered beams that looked like driftwood. When they walked up the stairs and to the elaborate porch,

66

Mackenzie noted the sign hanging in the single glass pane at the top of the double doors. It read: **This is a PRIVATE resort. If you belong here, you know it. And if you don't, kindly respect our privacy.**

"Not even any contact information," Ellington pointed out.

Almost exactly like DCM, Mackenzie thought.

She knocked on the door and stepped back so she could see through the glass pane along the top of the door. When no one had answered twenty seconds later, she knocked again. This time, someone showed up to the window almost immediately. An irritated-looking man peered through the glass at them. He then pointed to the sign in the glass, as if they had maybe just missed it.

In response, Mackenzie nodded and then showed her badge. She pressed it to the glass for emphasis. When she removed it, she saw the look of confusion on the man's face. He stepped back, opened the door, and stepped out onto the porch to meet them. He closed the door behind him and stood in front of it, making it clear that they would not be invited inside.

He was in his late forties, graying hair and a beard outlining his face. He looked rather gaunt, almost *too* skinny.

"Can I help you?" he asked, skeptically looking at Mackenzie's ID as she returned it to the inner pocket of her jacket.

"Yes, we were hoping to speak with the individual that operates and maintains a club known as Tidal Hills," Mackenzie said.

"Well, that would be Samuel," the man said. "And Tidal Hills is no *club*."

"Is Samuel here?" Mackenzie asked, ignoring the man's last barb.

"He is, but he is quite busy. He is meditating and preparing for an event tonight."

"We need to speak with him," Mackenzie said.

"I'm afraid I can't allow you in while he's in preparations."

"Fine," Mackenzie said. "Have him come out here to us then. I'll give you three minutes. And if he's not out here, we're coming in to speak with him."

The man nodded quickly, reaching back for the door handle. He still looked irritated but he also looked very worried. He opened the door and returned inside very quickly. Mackenzie noted that in his haste, he had not locked the door back behind him. She chose to stay outside, though, not wanting to antagonize a potential source without just cause.

"That guy looked sick," Ellington said.

"Thin as a rail," Mackenzie agreed.

"Isolated, quiet, and not seen from the road," Ellington said. "Seems more like a cult than a club, don't you think?"

"Yeah, it has that vibe."

They stood and waited for another minute until the rail-thin man returned. He opened the door and peered out at them. "Samuel has invited you inside. Please come in."

He opened the door for them and they stepped inside. They entered a darkened room that resembled a church sanctuary, only without the pews and religious symbols. The thin man led them through this room, toward a door in the back. He turned to them with an uncertain smile and said, "This is a privilege, believe me. It is not often that Samuel invites non-members into his private space."

Wow, this is *starting to seem more and more like a cult,* Mackenzie thought. She and Ellington shared a look that conveyed *can you believe this?* Ellington shook his head, hiding an uneasy smile.

The thin man opened the door in the back and led them into a small hallway. The hallway contained six doors, all of which were opened except one. This was at the far end of the hallway—the exact door the thin man was leading them toward.

When they reached the door, the man knocked and again gave them an excited sort of smile. He then opened it and revealed a bare room with only a carpet for decoration. Three candles burned in the back of the room, illuminating the figure of a man that sat in the center of the rug.

"Please," the man said. "Come inside, visitors."

Mackenzie walked into the room, overwhelmed by two things: a creepy sensation that washed over her like a wave, and the fact that the man on the rug was naked except for a very tight pair of silk boxer briefs. The man—Samuel, if she was guessing correctly—looked to be in his fifties. Like the thin man, he also looked nearly malnourished...which was odd, given the defined abs and toned muscles in his arms and legs. He was sitting on the rug with his legs crossed and his back slightly arched.

When the thin man closed the door behind him and took his leave, the man got to his knees and then into a standing position. He did not seem to be bothered by his lack of attire.

"Nice to meet you both," he said. "I am Samuel, the guru of Tidal Hills."

"We're Agents White and Ellington with the FBI," Mackenzie said. "And I'll admit my confusion...what do you mean by *guru*?"

"I do my very best to lead my friends and members to peace through enlightenment and the proper way to embrace pleasure."

"Pleasure," Ellington said. "You mean sexual acts?"

"Yes. And any other pleasures of the flesh. Whereas most religions teach their followers that sex is to be a thing of shame and guilt, we here at Tidal Hills embrace it. We believe the act of sex and the intimacy derived from it can lead humans to an enlightened state."

"With all due respect," Mackenzie said, "we've heard that there are people that use Tidal Hills as a makeshift swingers' club."

Samuel frowned at the insinuation but nodded. "Yes, I could see how some might think such a thing. In my early days, that's how it got started. This was a place for people to come explore their sexuality, to expand their appetites. And somehow that turned into married couples wanting to engage with other married couples. It became the trend here and we embraced it."

"And is that still how things work here?"

"Yes. But it's not just married couples. We still have singles from time to time, wanting to find answers about their own sexuality."

"Your friend said you rarely have visitors," Mackenzie asked. "Why is that?"

"The majority of the world does not understand the intent we have here. Some see it as sinful and disgusting. Others sort of understand it but label it as a form of pornography. And what we do here is neither."

"He also said you were preparing for an event," Ellington said. "What did he mean?"

"We have a gathering later tonight. I like to meditate and prepare my body."

"Do you take part in these events?" Mackenzie asked.

Samuel paused for just a beat before answering. "When I am asked and I feel it is appropriate, yes."

Mackenzie felt the conversation taking several strange turns so she did her best to get it back on track.

"Samuel, we're here as part of an investigation into a string of murders that involve married couples," she said. "We've recently learned that one of the couples in question were once members here."

"Oh my. Might I ask who they were?"

"Josh and Julie Kurtz. Do you remember them?"

"I do," he said, his face slackening. "They did not stay with us long. I believe the wife in particular was not wholly receptive to our practices."

"And when they left, was it amicable?" she asked.

"Oh yes. Anytime anyone wants to leave, they are welcome to. All we ask is that they don't share specific details about what takes place here."

"Did the Kurtzes have any altercations with anyone here?"

"No, quite the opposite. They were such a lovely couple. Very nice, very sweet."

"How many couples do you consider members of Tidal Hills?"

"Right now, I believe we have fifteen active couples and seven singles."

"Is there a fee to join?" Ellington asked.

"Yes. However, I'm sure you understand that due to privacy, I'd rather not give you any specifics."

"Of course," Ellington responded dryly.

"Of the couples that are currently members, do you know them all?" Mackenzie asked.

"Yes, I know them all quite well."

"Have you ever had issues with any of them? Anything alarming about them?"

"No, not currently."

"Do you have any way of knowing if any of your current members have dabbled in other clubs or events for swingers?"

"That I do not know," Samuel said. "And I make it my business not to know. Any members go through a rigorous interview process with me. But in that process, while I do ask them about their history and their sex lives, I do not ask them anything like that. It is their business where they spend their time and money. I do not cross that line."

"So you can't think of a single person that might have come off as maybe resistant to your ways? Or maybe someone you had to turn away from being a member?"

Samuel thought about this, looking thoughtfully at one of the dancing candle flames. "You know, there was a young man about a year and a half ago. He made it through the interview process easily enough. Seemed like a fine young man. But when he came to his first event, I think it overwhelmed him. He did not cause a big fuss, but he left that night calling us all names. Called us perverts and said we were going to Hell. He contacted me later, apologizing and asking to rejoin, but I refused."

"Anything else?"

70

"Well, he's phoned me several times and keeps emailing me. He's come here one time in the last few months, banging on the door. Each time he contacted me, he seemed a bit more hostile."

"Do you think he's a danger?" Mackenzie.

"I don't know. He was rejected. Jilted. But in one of his emails, he vowed to get even with me."

"Could we have his name?"

Samuel seemed at odds with the idea but when he let out a defeated sigh, Mackenzie knew that he would give up the information.

"His name was Chino Castillo. I can give you his number, email address, and physical address—assuming he's still living in the same place, of course. But this is a breach of privacy. I'd rather you not let him know where you got his information. Although, given the nature of your case, I assume it will be obvious."

Funny, Mackenzie thought. *So much emphasis on privacy with this guy and Gloria Benitez...not something you'd expect from people that promote open marriages and sex lives.*

"Thank you for your help," Mackenzie said.

"Of course," Samuel said, though it was evident that he was upset by the whole matter. He ushered them toward the door. He followed them out back down the hallway toward the large front room.

"You know," he said, "I am well aware of the stigma associated with what we do here. And I even understand it. But there is much more good than bad to come out of this. I welcome either of you to return without badges or guns and take part."

Mackenzie wasn't sure but she thought she heard Ellington stifle back a chuckle.

"I appreciate the offer," Mackenzie said, "but I don't think that would be the best idea. We're in the midst of a case and, quite frankly, it wouldn't sit well with our supervisors."

"I understand. And I certainly hope you wrap up your case quickly."

"Do you truly believe Chino Castillo would be capable of murdering people?"

"I honestly have no idea," Samuel said. "I didn't think he'd be capable of the anger he's expressed since being kicked out, but there it is anyway. Would it be okay if I text you his information?"

"Of course," Mackenzie said. She gave Samuel her number and added: "The sooner, the better."

"Oh, I'll have it to you within ten minutes."

Samuel led them back to the front doors, still dressed in only the tight silk boxers. The thin man was in the large room, laying out an assortment of mats on the floor. He gave them a nod and a wave as they passed.

Outside, Ellington seemed to be in a hurry to get to the car. When Mackenzie reached the car she found him laughing and shaking his head.

"Something funny?" she asked.

He looked at her, a little embarrassed. "I'm sorry. I know it's unprofessional. But between Samuel and the Springs couple, I think I've seen my fair share of nearly naked strangers today."

"It *has* been a bit much," she said. "But if seeing an aging bald man in his too-tight boxers is what it takes to get a lead…"

"Then it was time well spent," Ellington finished for her.

They drove away from Tidal Hills, the Miami skyline now cast in shadows as the sun had given up the fight, making way for the moon. To Mackenzie, all it meant was that yet another day had passed without finding the killer—and that the killer seemed farther away than ever, despite the new leads.

CHAPTER FIFTEEN

The music was blaring. It was some God-awful techno-pop that he could feel in his skull like daggers. He was drinking scotch to dull it but it wasn't doing any good. In fact, the more he drank, the more he seemed to be able to tolerate the music.

He knew that he couldn't drink much more. He'd already had two and he knew that five was his absolute limit. Not only did he need to be able to drive back home, but he also needed to keep his mind clear. He knew why he was here, but he was already pretty sure it was not going to work.

He wanted to forget about the things he'd done over the last week or so. But beyond that, he wanted to move on. He wanted to stop. And that's why he was here. He figured he might meet someone. No one special, just someone to spend the night with. Maybe another couple. Maybe he would be able to remember what the whole scene was supposed to be about.

Of course, this shitty dance club was not why he was here. He was here because he knew what happened in the upstairs parlor. It was a little-known secret—a secret he had been privy to for about two years now. He'd been twice, not nearly enough so that anyone in the club would recognize his face.

He sat alone at a small round table across from the club's secondary bar. He was sitting there because it offered him an unobstructed view to the stairway that led to the upstairs. He had seen three couples head up there within the last half hour. The event, he knew, started in about ten minutes. There was no one standing by the stairs to keep anyone from going up. But he knew there would be a few people in the hallway in front of the parlor that would keep any unwanted people from entering.

He also knew that you could not go up alone. You had to have at least one other person with you. It was a couples thing—a swingers thing. Sometimes there would be swinger events where singles could show up and get in the mix. Sometimes an extra body was needed, and that was fine.

But this was not one of those times.

As the time drew near, he found himself getting excited. He was not aroused, as he usually was. Tonight was not about the prospect of sex or even meeting someone that interested him. No, tonight was all about reconnecting…about remembering why he had ever gotten involved in a scene like this in the first place.

His hope was that it would help cleanse him. That it would help to get rid of the rage and perhaps even blot out the memories of the murders he had committed.

He downed his drink and left the table. He quickly settled up his tab with the bartender. The bar was crowded with people in their early twenties. The girls wore very little; there was probably more makeup on their bodies than clothes. He wondered how many of them knew what went on upstairs…and how they might react if they were presented with it.

He scoped out the scene without being too obvious. He counted five separate clusters of people—distinct groups within the bar. Most of them were paired up, but he did see one table with three people, two women and a man, that kept shooting glances over toward the stairs.

He checked his watch. The event began in ten minutes. If he was going to give this a shot, he had to do it now.

He walked over to the table with three people sitting at it and made no pretenses. He smiled as he approached, taking in the trio. The male was good-looking in an Abercrombie sort of way. His hair was slicked back and you could practically see his abs through his shirt. The women were easily no older than thirty and dressed as if they were only eighteen and were out of the house, on their own, for the first time ever. The woman to the right wasn't wearing a bra, made evident by the fact that her left breast was about to pop out of her top.

"You guys heading upstairs?" he asked.

All three of them instantly tensed up. The woman to the left gave the man an *eew, what the hell is this* sort of look.

"It's okay," he said. "I've been here before. I've been upstairs before. My girlfriend changed her mind at the last minute, though. I was looking to pair up with someone and head upstairs."

Most of this was true. The one false part was that he had a girlfriend who had bailed. He did not have a girlfriend. All he had was a very disgruntled ex-wife who had been getting laid behind his back for about a year before he found out about it.

"Nah, man," the guy said. "We're set here."

Almost as if an afterthought because they felt bad for him, the woman with a mostly exposed left breast nodded her head to the right. "But I think that table over there is looking for a guy."

He looked in that direction and bit back a frown. It was two guys and one girl. The girl looked drunk out of her mind (some of them needed that to get into what happened upstairs; he knew this from experience) and two older men. One of them was easily twenty years the girl's senior.

It was not an ideal situation; then again, if she was with older men, he doubted she was picky. And it wasn't like he was trying to hook up with her. He just wanted to be able to get in upstairs.

He walked over to the table. As he did, he saw movement beneath it. One of the men had his hands up the woman's skirt and wasn't being too discreet about it.

He nearly turned around right then and there. But he had to try. He had to make some sort of effort to reconnect…to make himself stop what he had been doing all week.

"Hey there," he said, being as friendly as he could as he approached the side of their table. It was mostly obscured by the dim lights of the bar.

"Hey yourself," said one of the men—the one who had his hands busy beneath the table.

"Look…I know it seems fishy, but my girlfriend just texted me. Said she can't make it. So I'm trying to find a group to latch on to so I can head upstairs."

Both men looked instantly appalled. They actually both seemed to scoot in closer to the woman. Meanwhile, she began to smile…a smile that eventually broke out into a laugh.

"Dude," she said. "Um…no. That's fucking creepy. We don't know you."

"Yeah," he said, trying to bite back his rage. "I understand that. But it's not like I'm new to this. I've been here before. This is not—"

"Don't care," she said. And although she was clearly drunk and her words were coming out without any sort of filter, they still stung. "That's gross. Don't act like you know us." She then kept laughing, slapping at the table and looking at him like he was an idiot.

"She's right," the older man said. "I'm not sure there's an actual etiquette for things like this, but if there were, things like this would be a violation I'm sure. Now please…step away before this just gets really awkward and weird."

Like the scene at your table and what you're about to do upstairs isn't awkward and weird, he thought to himself.

He wanted to hit them. He wished he had his knife. He felt his blood boiling and it took every ounce of restraint within him not to lash out. Especially at the drunk bitch while she was still laughing.

He sneered and turned around.

He was disappointed that he would not make it into the parlor upstairs. He was also upset that he had seemed so desperate. The woman had a right to laugh at him (though maybe not *so* much, given her choice of company). He was an embarrassment, and he had to understand that things would never be the way they had been before.

More than that, he was ashamed of himself for falling victim to the rage so easily.

He had truly hoped that he'd be able to exorcise his demons tonight—through sex, through losing himself to a stranger, to being a part of something that had made sense to him once upon a time.

But no…now all there was to feel was the hatred.

He knew how to expel it…how to get rid of it for a while. He didn't want to but he knew that if he didn't, it would only grow stronger. He had put it off as much as he could for a very long time…and when it had finally snapped…well, he had the images of the Carlsons' bloodied bodies to remind him of it.

He was going to have to do it again.

But how long can I keep it up? he wondered.

The answer was simple. And it seemed to soothe the rage inside of him.

For as long as it takes.

CHAPTER SIXTEEN

Mackenzie decided that because it was only 8:05, they'd be okay to pay Chino Castillo a visit. As it turned out, his home was directly on the way back to the precinct, about a thirty-minute drive from Tidal Hills. The city was nearly overtaken by the darkness of night when they reached his street. It was not a rundown section of town but it was far from the luxurious accommodations they'd seen at the Carlsons' and the Springses' homes.

When she parked in front of the address Samuel had given them, they spotted a man perched by the side of the house. He was hunkered down in front of a push lawnmower, scraping at the underside beyond the blade. He was working by the aid of the porch light which had collected a swarm of gnats and other bugs.

Mackenzie approached him slowly with Ellington behind her. The man looked up to them with a slightly concerned face.

"Are you Chino Castillo?" Mackenzie asked.

"Yeah, that's me. Who are you?"

Mackenzie went through her introductory act, giving their names and flashing her ID. "Your name was provided by someone we've spoken to concerning a case we're working on. We were hoping you had some time to speak with us."

"Sure," he said, although it was clear he was uneasy with the idea. He put the mower back down on its wheels and peeled off the gloves he had been using to scrape out the underside. "What's going on?"

"Well, we're looking for a suspect that has been involved with Tidal Hills as well as a private club known as DCM. We have it on good authority that you have had dealings with at least one of those places."

"That's right. Tidal Hills."

He went quiet then, as if waiting for them to tell him why that mattered. Mackenzie could tell that he was frightened. And while that was not necessarily an indication of guilt, it usually meant there was something in his life worth hiding.

"We understand that there were some issues," Mackenzie continued. "Have you been pestering the man who calls himself the guru?"

Chino scoffed at this as he led Mackenzie and Ellington up onto his porch. "Is that what this is about? Did that prick complain about me?"

"He *did* complain about you," Mackenzie said. "But that was not the point of our visit. We were questioning him about the same case we are asking you about. During our questioning, your name came up."

"What a joke," Chino said.

"Well, that's what we're hoping," Mackenzie said. "But just to clear up the stories, could you tell us what happened?"

Chino looked at the boards of his porch as he plopped down in a rickety old lawn chair. "Yeah, but it's embarrassing in hindsight. See, I had this friend that had heard about what they do at Tidal Hills. Some sort of spiritual junk, but really it's about sex. Some excuse to have orgies or partner-swapping. And I had been going through a dry spell...had a bad run with getting almost addicted to porn. So I gave it a try. I went down there and Samuel put me through this ridiculously extensive interview process, and I was in."

"How long were you a member?" Ellington asked.

"About a week," Chino said. "I went one night and nothing really happened. I hooked up with this one woman but it didn't go very far. I just...I don't know. I wasn't ready for it. I got freaked out. So we made out for a while and then left the room where everything was going down. We hung out on the porch outside the building and just talked."

"Did you ever return?" Mackenzie asked.

"Yeah. One more time. My last night as a member, I guess. I wasn't there for very long. I hooked back up with the woman I had met the first time. We were fooling around but...the way they do things...everyone is screwing in front of everyone else. It's this big open space. I think there are private rooms that Samuel uses, but I never saw those. Anyway, me and this woman, we were about to start actually having sex. But it was just too weird for me. So I stopped. I started putting my clothes back on."

"And did Samuel call you out for that?"

"Not at first. I don't think he even noticed at first. He was over on the other side of the room, watching this group of people go at it. But someone saw me leaving and made this really crude comment. Said I was a perv. Someone else called me a virgin. I argued back and when Samuel *did* finally get involved, he asked me to leave. He was very rude about it, too. So I told him to go fuck himself and then got out of there. And I never went back."

"Well," Mackenzie said, "Samuel claims that you have been harassing him. He says you're begging him to become a member again."

"Seriously? Well, that's just a blatant lie."

"He says you've sent emails," Mackenzie said.

"More lies," he said. "You're welcome to have a look at my computer. Do whatever you need to do."

"Thank you for that," Mackenzie said. "If nothing really pans out, we may have to take you up on that. In the meantime, tell me…while you were at Tidal Hills, did you ever meet a couple named the Kurtzes?"

Chino thought about this for a while and then shook his head. "Not that I know of. The only person I really ever spoke to was the woman I nearly hooked up with. And to be quite honest, I don't remember her name. Anna, maybe? Annette?"

"Is there anything else you can tell us about Tidal Hills itself?" Ellington asked.

Chino shrugged. "I've tried to forget about it. It was creepy. I know they parade themselves around as this exclusive spiritual retreat, but that's nonsense. It's an excuse to have orgies. That's it. It's like a sex cult almost. Samuel tries to weave bullshit meditation and awakening into it, but that's about five minutes at the beginning. And by then, people are already partnering up with each other."

Mackenzie nodded. She'd also gotten a creepy vibe from just being around Samuel. If there *had* been something strange taking place there when the Kurtzes had been members, maybe there was some digging left to do.

"Any abuse taking place?" Mackenzie asked.

"I don't know," he said. "Samuel, though…he had this weird way of convincing people he was this chilled-out guru. The women went nuts for him. On the night I left, he was watching three people go at it while two other women were pawing at him. It's disgusting. The woman I was messing around with…she even said that she'd heard from other women that there were no interviews for them. They just had to audition for him."

"Audition?" Ellington asked.

"Yeah," Chino said. "Use your imagination."

Mackenzie had heard enough. She was thoroughly disgusted and rather pissed at herself that Samuel had played her so well.

Maybe I was just so creeped out and eager to get out of there, she thought. *But that creep is definitely up to something.*

"And you have never called him or anything?" Mackenzie asked.

"God no," Chino said. He reached into his pocket and removed his phone. He handed it over to her and said, "You're welcome to check this, too. Computer, phone, anything."

Mackenzie took his phone after Chino punched in his passcode. She scrolled through his contacts, emails, photos, everything. She saw nothing that instantly linked him to Samuel.

"You'd be okay for us to call the phone company and go through your records?"

"If you have to," Chino said. "Anything you need to do to prove that I have no connections to that asshole, you have my permission."

Mackenzie nodded and handed his phone back to him.

"I don't think that will be necessary," she said. "Mr. Castillo, thanks so much for your time and willingness to help."

"No problem," he replied. "I'm just glad he's being exposed for what he is."

Mackenzie didn't see the point in arguing that Samuel wasn't the object of their interest. However, now that she was pretty sure he had blatantly lied to them, he sure as hell was now.

She and Ellington headed back to the car. As they glanced at one another over the roof before getting in, Ellington said: "We heading back to Tidal Hills?"

"Yep."

"Taking Samuel up on his invitation to join in?"

"Nope."

"You're no fun," he joked.

"Shut up and get in the car."

As she pulled back out, once again heading for Tidal Hills, she started to feel a sense of progress. The Kurtzes were connected to Samuel, even if in a very small way. And now that she had caught Samuel in a pretty extensive lie, she couldn't help but wonder what other information he might be hiding.

Maybe, if they were lucky, a clear and direct path to a killer.

CHAPTER SEVENTEEN

Mackenzie had made some very awkward arrests in the past. But as they neared Tidal Hills for a second time, she tried to imagine what it might be like to arrest a man while orchestrating a strange and cult-like orgy. The concept did not sit well with her, which was why she was very grateful when they arrived back at the location before anything had the chance to get properly started.

As before, the front door was locked. She wasted no time, hammering on it with her fist. She could hear multiple murmuring voices the other side. She could even see a few people looking toward the glass along the top of the door—a few middle-aged women and a younger male. They looked confused, maybe even a little worried.

Finally, after she had hammered on the door for roughly fifteen seconds, it was answered. It was the same scrawny man from before. He looked irritated but she also saw fear in his eyes. It had not been there the first time she'd seen him. It was the sort of expression that was very telling. Just seeing it as he opened the door for her told her that someone—maybe not him, but certainly someone he knew—was guilty of something.

He opened the door and did his best to appear defiant. "I'm sorry, Agents. We're in the middle of a meeting here and—"

"From what I can see," Mackenzie said, "everyone still has their clothes on. So I'll do my very best to get in and out before anything too disgusting happens."

"But you can't just—"

Mackenzie stepped forward, making it clear that if she had to, she'd roll right over him. He stepped aside, allowing both of them into the entryway. They walked into the large open room they had been inside less than an hour and a half ago. Mackenzie took a quick count of the room as she walked toward the front, where Samuel was standing on a raised platform. She counted twenty-two people in all. Most of the women were clearly not wearing bras beneath their shirts; she assumed most also went sans panties beneath their shorts and skirts.

She made it halfway through the crowd before Samuel started to speak from the stage.

"Sorry, friends," he said, apologizing to the gathered crowd. "It appears that some people simply have no regard for privacy."

81

Mackenzie smirked at him as she reached the little stage. She kept her voice low so only he could hear it, doing her best to remain as professional as possible.

"And it appears that some *others*," she said, "have no regard for being truthful with federal agents."

Samuel gave his audience an apologetic *what are you gonna do* sort of smile and then leaned in closer to Mackenzie. "Agent White, I don't know what you're talking about but I can assure you this is neither the time nor the place."

"Oh, I'm sure this room full of consenting adults is fully capable of banging one another without you looking over them," she said. "Besides...if you can produce evidence that Chino Castillo either emailed or called you, I'll leave. More than that, I'll apologize to your friends here and let them know the mistake was mine."

She read his face as his eyes darted back and forth, looking for a way out of it. When he finally replied, it was the final bit of intangible proof she needed of guilt.

"And if I don't?" he asked.

"Then you'll be escorted off the premises in FBI custody. If you don't make too much of a scene, I'll maybe even give you the dignity of not having to wear cuffs in front of your horny masses."

"I don't have the evidence on me."

"Neither did Chino Castillo," she countered. "The only difference is that I looked through his phone and he was more than willing to have me go through his phone records for proof. He encouraged it, in fact. So...I need that proof."

"I. Don't. Have. It."

Mackenzie had to bite back a grin. She almost felt bad about how easily she had gotten under his skin. She glanced back at Ellington and saw that he was standing in the back of the room with the skinny doorman.

"Then I'm going to have to ask you to come with us," she said.

"That's not going to happen," he said. He was still whispering, but he was growing more and more agitated.

"If you don't step down off of this stage right now, I'm going to have to escort you myself. And then what would all of these eager women think? Seeing you manhandled by a mere little woman?"

"You wouldn't da—"

He wasn't able to finish getting out the word *dare*. Mackenzie quickly grabbed his left arm and swung out lightly. When he lost his footing, she then pulled him to her and twisted the arm up. The

82

whole move took less than two seconds. When it was over, Samuel was on the ground with Mackenzie kneeling on top of him, a knee on his back.

A few people came rushing forward to assist their guru.

From the back, Ellington roared out: "FBI! Anyone else moves another step towards my partner and you can spend some time with your fearless leader here in the back of our car on the way to an interrogation room."

Everyone stopped right away, giving curious and concerned glances all around the room.

Mackenzie hauled Samuel back to his feet and instantly started to push him forward. Mackenzie saw looks of shock and sadness on some of their faces and actually felt bad for them. What sort of lies had Samuel told them? How, exactly, had he manipulated them?

Maybe they enjoy it, she thought as she pushed him through the crowd, toward the back of the room. *And maybe Samuel knew that…and exploited it.*

Whatever the reason, she led him out of the building in absolute silence as the stunned people in attendance looked on.

* * *

As the day wound down closer to midnight, Samuel was placed in an interrogation room. While Mackenzie and Ellington worked out the details of their visit to Tidal Hills with Rodriguez and others on his force, a small team was tasked with looking into Samuel's background.

As it turned out, there was quite a lot to report. Several pages of information were handed to Mackenzie as she and Ellington fueled up on a late-night cup of coffee. They looked over them together as she started to feel the first signs of tiredness sweeping over her. She was more than accustomed to working long days and had learned to fight it off for a while. She knew that, if need be, she could go another six to eight hours without needing to crash for a bit.

The brief report they had been handed told a quick yet rather lewd story. The man labeling himself as a "guru" was Samuel Netti. He was fifty-three years old and had been a resident of Miami or surrounding areas for twenty years or so. Beforehand, he had lived in Houston, Texas, where he had started to amass a rocky record. He'd been arrested twice for being caught with prostitutes. He also had a single domestic charge against him, filed by a woman he had been engaged to for a period of four months.

He then came to Miami, where he had been audited by the IRS (and come out clean in the end) and had been the subject of speculation in a case involving a small prostitution ring. All of the women questioned, however, gave enough evidence to clear him. Whispers of his involvement in an exclusive spa or club of some kind had been passed around the city but not taken seriously.

"Sounds like a classy guy," Ellington said, standing up from the table. He downed his coffee and rolled his head on his neck, loosening up the muscles.

"Yeah," Mackenzie said. "A real winner."

They left the break room and informed Rodriguez that they were ready to question Samuel Netti. Rodriguez, who also looked very tired, walked with them to the room and gave them full control.

"I'll be watching with a few of my men," he said. "Let us know what we can do to help."

When he was out of earshot and heading into the observation room, Ellington said: "You want good cop or bad cop?"

"Both," she said, and walked inside.

Samuel looked up at them with disdain. The fear and uncertainty was no longer in his eyes. He had apparently accepted his position and was going to try his best to remain calm.

Good, she thought. *I'd like to be out of his presence as soon as possible.*

She typically did not like to lie to suspects; she felt it weakened her argument, particularly if the suspect was able to trip her up. Still, in this case, she felt certain that Samuel had lied to them and, consequently, Chino Castillo had told them the truth.

"Here's the deal," she said. "The phone records are in. There have been absolutely zero calls made from Chino Castillo's phone to your cell phone. The emails seem to check out, too. So tell me why you lied to us about him."

The worry that flashed across his face told Mackenzie that her suspicions were dead on. Samuel sighed and looked at both of them with a resigned expression.

"Because I wanted you out of my hair," he said. "I figured you were just another couple of cops that had found out about what we do at Tidal Hills and were looking into it."

"That's called *feeling guilty,*" Mackenzie said. "That and your sordid past in Houston would keep you paranoid, I suppose. But one would think it would also cause you to be smart enough to not lie to federal agents. Also, even when you learned why we were really there, you decided to lie. Why is that? Did you have something against Chino Castillo?"

"Of course I did. He came in twice, got an eyeful, and then left. I have a very strong no-voyeur policy. And that's what he was doing. Fortunately, that is the only time such a thing has ever occurred at Tidal Hills. Having him out there, having seen what goes on inside…it makes me very uncomfortable."

"And what *does* go on inside?" Ellington asked. "From what Castillo tells us, there's very little spirituality taking place and a whole lot of fucking."

Samuel actually looked as if someone had reached out and slapped him hard across the face. The obscenity had apparently taken him by complete surprise, nearly disgusting him.

"That's not true. It's—"

No, I think it is," Mackenzie said. "And while it makes me sick, there's technically nothing illegal about it. Of course, I have no idea how you spend the money people pay you for fees or anything like that. Although, I'm sure that might be worth looking into."

"Look, what do you want from me?" Samuel asked.

"I need to know about the Kurtzes," Mackenzie said.

"In that regard, I was not lying. They were not with me for very long and when they left, it was amicable. No hostility. From what I remember, they were very nice. Quite kind and funny from what I remember."

"And no bad vibes with anyone else?" Mackenzie asked.

"No. If they did, it happened behind the scenes and I never knew about it."

Mackenzie had been pacing up until now. She finally took a seat in front of the same table Samuel was sitting at.

"You sure about that?" Mackenzie asked, even though she was pretty sure he was telling the truth. "It seems to me that a man as popular as you within such a small circle would hear just about everything."

"Yes, I swear it," Samuel said. She could hear the pleading in his voice. He was apparently sensing that she and Ellington were already running low on avenues to use in their interrogation.

"What about the auditions?" Mackenzie asked. "Have you ever allowed a woman to audition for a spot in your little club?"

"Audition?"

Mackenzie got back to her feet. She knew the path she was headed down had nothing to do with the case. But God, she hated this man.

"You knowingly lied when an FBI agent asked you a question," she said. "There are criminal charges attached to that. Usually you can get off with a fine or slap on the wrist. But with your preexisting record—"

"Look. I don't know anything else about these Kurtzes," he said. "I swear. If you want, I can ask some of the other members but I honestly don't know."

She looked at him, trying to tell if he was being honest. She was pretty sure he was but she also felt her resentment and anger toward him rising up like flames in her heart. She turned her back on him and started for the door.

"You good?" Ellington asked as she passed him.

"Just need a second," she said.

Without another word or any explanation, she left the interrogation room. She stood between the doors of the interrogation room and the observation room, leaning back against the cinderblock wall.

It was rare that a suspect got to her for such obscure reasons. Samuel Netti had not hurt her or affected anyone she knew. It was simply his character—a man that was skilled at manipulating women and using the nature of human sexuality to his advantage.

All of that is true, she thought. *But there's something else there, Mac. You know it. You feel it...so what the hell is it?*

In her mind's eye, she saw the beds of the murdered couples. She thought about someone the couples knew coming into the house and killing them.

Just like with Dad, she thought.

And that was it. At the heart of it all, Samuel Netti would usually not bother her any more than some other random sexual deviant. But the fact that this case was echoing her father's own case had her worked up more than she cared to admit.

Get a grip, she told herself. *This is just like any other case and, as of right now, you're still mostly in the dark.*

She took a series of deep breaths and started back for the door. As she did so, the door to the observation room flew open. Rodriguez came rushing out, his cell phone held up to his ear. He looked very alarmed, almost excited.

"Agent White," he said, his voice edged with worry. "There's been another murder."

"A couple?"

"Yes."

"Where?"

"Where is it again?" Rodriguez asked whoever was on the other end of the line. After a few seconds, and a very confused look, Rodriguez said, "Thanks," and then ended the call.

"Where is it?" Mackenzie asked.

"Well, it's weird as hell…but these bodies are on a cruise ship."

"Is it on the water or docked?"

"On the water. But it's coming back to port as we speak."

"So the murders occurred while it was at sea?"

"No way to know," Rodriguez said. "But we *do* know that these bodies are fresh. They were likely killed within the last several hours."

Suddenly, Mackenzie did not feel the creeping fingers of exhaustion creeping in. With a fresh murder and a confined area, this case just got much more accessible.

She opened the interrogation room door, ignoring Samuel Netti completely. Her eyes found Ellington and she saw that he was registering her excitement.

"Come on," she told him. "It looks like we've got a ship to catch."

CHAPTER EIGHTEEN

At Mackenzie's instruction, no one was allowed to leave the cruise ship. As a result, she saw hundreds of people milling around the decks as she parked her car in the cruise line's luggage and equipment lot alongside the ship's docking platform. Two patrol cars from the Miami PD rolled into the lot behind her. They were not running their sirens or flashers, not wanting to further alarm the passengers. As far as Mackenzie knew, none of the passengers had been informed of why the cruise had been turned back to shore just a few hours after heading out to sea.

Mackenzie walked toward the ship entrance she had been instructed to. There, a man with a rather rotund belly hanging over the waist of his jeans stood waiting for her. When he saw Mackenzie and Ellington headed their way with Rodriguez and a few of his officers behind them, he walked toward them with his hand extended for a shake.

"Hi, Agents," this man said. "I'm Bill Hudson, head of ship security."

Introductions were made all around and then Hudson quickly escorted them onto the ship. Inside, three other members of ship security joined them, along with Rodriguez and the five officers he had tasked to come along. At first Mackenzie thought so many people would be overkill, although she *had* requested a few of Rodriguez's men to help with questioning duties when it came to speaking to all of the passengers.

But as soon as they made their way out of the loading area and cargo holds and onto the decks, she was glad they had the extra bodies. Several of the security members and the Miami PD had to part a lane for her and Ellington to walk through down a small corridor that led to the ship's central elevator.

Mackenzie and Ellington went up with Rodriguez and Hudson while the other officers and security members remained on the lower floors. It wasn't until they were out of the elevator and walking down the long and narrow hallway of the third floor that Hudson started to talk. Even then, he spoke in whispers despite the fact that all passengers had been asked to vacate the third floor upon docking.

"We had security and most of the crew call all passengers out to the decks for the safety briefings," Hudson said. "Standard stuff. We do it on all cruises. And we stress it really hard—so much so that we have crew members go through every floor, knocking on every door to ensure everyone takes part. But, honestly, it's also something we do to make sure there's nothing shady going on. It lets us snoop around the hallways while everyone else is out on the decks."

Hudson came to a stop at room 341 and took a keycard out of his pocket. He did not insert it yet, though. With a heavy tone to his voice, he continued. "One of our room service crew members checked this room during the safety briefing and found the bodies. Just to let you guys know…it's pretty gruesome. I've never seen anything like it, so this is new to me."

With that, he slipped the keycard in and opened the door.

Mackenzie and Ellington stepped inside first. Rodriguez followed behind them with Hudson trailing reluctantly behind. The room was small, as were most cruise line rooms, but tidy. The exception, of course, was the bed. Like the other three beds Mackenzie had seen at crime scenes in the last two days, it was a disarray of sheets and blood.

She approached the bed cautiously. The blood was still fresh so it glistened wetly in the soft overhead glow of the cabin's lights. She was about to ask Hudson the identity of the victims but found that she didn't need to.

"Shit," she breathed. "Ellington…"

"Yeah," he said, sidling up beside her. "I recognize them, too."

It made no sense and seemed rather unreal, but Mackenzie was looking down at the very recently murdered bodies of Jack and Vanessa Springs.

***

Her mind reeled with the realization as a million thoughts seemed to go racing through her head. As she took in the scene, now also noticing splatters of blood on the carpet and walls, she glanced back into her memory, trying to recall everything the Springses had told them. Had they mentioned a cruise? Had they mentioned a vacation?

No, she thought. *But Vanessa* did *tell me that they had another swinging event coming up very soon.*

"Mr. Hudson, what's the nature of this cruise?"

"Just a normal Caribbean cruise," he answered. "Three days and two nights. Adults only."

"Were there any privatized events scheduled?"

"No. It's just the usual cruise fare. Shuffleboard, dancing, mixology courses, things like that. What are you looking for, exactly?"

Rodriguez pulled out his phone and started texting someone. "I'm checking with the station," he told them. "Maybe there's a history of swinging events on these cruises."

"Swinging?" Hudson asked. "What do you m—wait. Swinging…like sex stuff?"

"Yes," Mackenzie said. "Had you heard rumors of anything like that?"

"No. I mean…that's sort of taboo, right? Are there cruises that actually do that?"

"I doubt they advertise it," Ellington said. "But apparently, yes."

Hudson seemed to dwell on this as Mackenzie continued to take in the scene. Like the other scenes, it was apparent a knife was used. There was no precision, no art to it; it had simply been a savage and violent act.

She saw a few drops of blood splattered on the carpet, including one that sat just below the bathroom door. She walked over to it and opened the door. Inside, two hand towels lay on the floor. One of them was matted in blood. A few toiletries from a fallen travel bag were also on the floor.

"Evidence of a struggle in here," she said.

Ellington and Rodriguez came over to have a look while Mackenzie returned her attention to Hudson.

"On a cruise like this, who would be the one that plans the events that take place onboard?"

"The events coordinator. She's speaking with the captain right now, trying to sort through the mess of having to turn back around."

"Can you please bring her to me?" she asked. "I'd like to speak with her."

"Of course," he said. "Give me five minutes."

He left quickly, already pulling his phone out of his pocket to place a call. Mackenzie returned her attention to the Springses. Jack was completely nude. Vanessa wore a yellow bikini that was mostly covered in blood. She saw that Jack's hand had been placed on Vanessa's thigh.

A carbon copy of the other crime scenes, she thought. *But on a cruise ship, they might have answered the door for anyone. Still…the killer has to be on the ship somewhere.*

It was an exciting thought, but there was yet another that halted it. She went back to the bathroom. She couldn't see where much of anything had been taken out of the travel bag before it had spilled. Nothing was on the small counters or sink. She went back out into the room and looked into the drawers. They were all empty. Their suitcases sat along the far wall, with the identification tags still on the handles, placed there when checking in for the cruise.

"What are you looking for?" Ellington asked her.

"Evidence that they had unpacked," she said. "I'm trying to get a gauge on when they were killed—at sea or before the boat even pulled away from the platform."

"You're thinking the killer acted before the chip departed?" Rodriguez asked.

"It's a possibility," she said.

It was depressing to hear it coming out of her mouth. Just like that, the hope of the case being simplified by having the killer isolated on a cruise ship was dashed. While she wasn't quite back to square one, it felt like it.

And the more she looked, the more certain she became that the Springses had been killed shortly after arriving in their room. Vanessa had just enough time to change into her bikini. Being that Jack was naked, Mackenzie assumed he had been attacked in the bathroom while getting ready to change. That or his being nude was some sort of symbolic gesture made by the killer—a gesture that Mackenzie could not yet decode.

As she tracked the blood on the floor and the bathroom, she got a better picture of what had happened. One of the Springses—presumably the nude Jack—had been killed in the restroom and then moved to the bed so they could be posed in this carbon copy pose that had been present at the other scenes. The killer had come in invited and left without any of the other hurried occupants of the third floor any wiser.

Hudson came back into the room with a frantic-looking woman trailing behind him. She was dressed in crew member attire and looked to be in her early fifties.

"Agents, this is Dana Crosby, the events coordinator," Hudson said.

Mackenzie wanted to waste no time. If the killer had managed to get off of the boat before it embarked on its brief journey, time was literally slipping away with every second.

"Mrs. Crosby, I'm wondering if there were any private events scheduled for this cruise."

"Yes, there was, actually," she said. "I was looking into it when Bill called me. It was just a reunion of some childhood friends, I believe."

"And did money have to pass hands to book such an event?"

"Yes. Five thousand dollars was paid per night to have the lower decks club for two hours on both nights."

"How many people were supposed to take part in that event?" Mackenzie asked.

"In the neighborhood of sixty people," she said. "Mostly married couples, I believe. I'm working to get a full list of those attending. The Springses were among them, though. I know that for sure."

"And who paid you the five thousand dollars per night?" Mackenzie asked.

"Well, the money didn't come to me. I was just the liaison. But booking and scheduling was my duty."

"Did you meet the person that booked the club?"

"Yes. She's currently being questioned by some of Bill's security guys. As I was coming down to meet with you, I believe I saw some of the police also heading her way."

"Where is she right now?"

"On the pool deck on the top floor."

"Could you take me to her?"

They made their way back out into the corridor and packed into the elevator. Things felt rushed and hurried as their little group went up: Mackenzie, Ellington, Crosby, Rodriguez, and Hudson. But that was fine with Mackenzie. Working at a fast pace made her feel like she was getting somewhere. Even when they stepped off on the upper pool deck and the suspicious glances of the ship's attendants fell on her, she felt like their gazes were pushing her along, closer to closing this case.

Dana Crosby led them to where several uniformed men were speaking with a young woman. She was quite striking, her blonde hair falling perfectly along the sides of her face and over her shoulders. She was dressed in a bathing suit that wasn't quite as tight and revealing as the one Vanessa Springs had died in. Mackenzie guessed her to be in her early thirties.

Mackenzie made her way through the small crowd of security officers and policemen. She showed her ID quickly, watching as Ellington did the same beside her.

"I'm Agent Mackenzie White," she said quickly. "I understand that you had organized some sort of event to take place during the cruise. Is that correct?"

"Am I in some sort of trouble?" the woman asked.

"Not if you're honest with us. We believe the murders onboard are directly related to a sensitive case. I have no time to waste and honestly won't tolerate anything less than cooperation. So please don't try to paint a prettier picture than the one I need to see. This event...what was it *really*?"

The woman frowned and Mackenzie realized that she had not even asked for the woman's name. She corrected this immediately, not wanting to seem impersonal and cold. "What's your name?" she asked.

"Alexa Myers."

"Alexa...listen. The couple that was murdered...I know the sort of things they were into. So just tell the truth. As long as you aren't connected to them in any real way, your involvement with this can end right here by this pool."

With a sigh, Alexa nodded and said: "It was a swingers event. We called it Coupling Couples. It was an invite-only kind of thing."

"And how was it decided who would be invited?"

"I got hooked on this whole thing awhile ago and somehow ended up being the sort of leader of a group of swingers. We started having two events a year—usually at my house, but, as it got bigger, at private venues."

"And I assume this is what you had rented the club below decks for?" Mackenzie asked.

"Yes."

Mackenzie turned to Dana Crosby. "Did you have any idea about this?"

"Absolutely not." The disgust on her face was genuine. Mackenzie believed her and sort of pitied her.

"Alexa, I need a list of everyone onboard that was invited to that event."

"I...I can't," she said. "I have to respect their privacy."

"Was there a contract signed?" Mackenzie asked.

"No."

"Then that's a non-issue. Mrs. Crosby has people running around the ship, trying to put a list together. But if you could just hand over a list, you'd save us hours of work and potentially help us get that much closer to catching a killer."

Alexa looked all around the deck, then glanced up to the darkness of the night sky. "Shit," she said.

"Alexa?"

"It's in my room."

"I'll escort you to get it," she said. "Mr. Hudson, would you mind coming along as well?"

Bill Hudson, also looking rather disgusted (but maybe a little intrigued, too) nodded. Alexa led them away from the pool and back to the elevators. Mackenzie looked back down the deck to where Ellington was speaking with Rodriguez and, behind him, the ship's guests mingled in a nervous chatter.

She glanced at her watch and saw that it was 1:07 in the morning.

Looks like it's going to be a sleepless night. She stepped into the elevator with Alexa and Hudson and they headed down. She wondered if the killer had used this elevator. She wondered if the killer knew Alexa.

And worse than all of that, she wondered how far away the killer was, escaping through the streets of Miami, while she was chasing her own tail on a cruise ship.

CHAPTER NINETEEN

While Mackenzie had accompanied Alexa to her cabin, Ellington had been working with Rodriguez and some of the other members of Bill Hudson's security team. When they all reconvened in Hudson's small and cramped quarters below deck, Mackenzie had a printout of the participants of Alexa's swinging event. Meanwhile, Ellington had learned a few rather depressing things about the ship's security system—mainly that there wasn't much of a system at all.

There were three cameras on each floor. They were positioned in a way that captured the length of each arm of the hallways. There were a few others on the pool decks and in the large lobby that connected the four different dining locations, but that was all. Really, though, that was all they needed.

Hudson pulled up the feed from the camera along the stretch of hall where room 341 was located. As he rewound the footage to go all the way back to when the Springses entered their room for the first time, Mackenzie started looking over Alexa's list. Alexa, who had been asked to come along in the off-chance that their camera footage revealed anything and she might be able to provide a name to go with a face, stood at the opened doorway of Hudson's office. She was quite nervous but seemed to be holding herself together well.

While looking over the list, she kept an eye out for any familiar names: *Kurtz, Sterling, Carlson.* None of them showed up.

About halfway down the sheet, she saw where Alexa had marked through a set of names with a black marker.

"What's this name right here?" she asked, pointing to the crossed-out listing.

"The O'Learys," Alexa said. "Nice enough people but there's been a rumor circulating that Devin, the husband, has HIV. I wanted to get the news for myself, so I tried getting in touch with them. But he's not taking my calls or answering my emails."

"And what about the wife?"

"Well, according to the rumors, she left him. He contracted HIV through an affair. I can't stress enough that these are rumors. But I kept his name on there, just in case. But then about a week ago, he finally answered one of my emails."

"So these were just rumors?"

"At first, yes…that was what I thought."

"How well do you know your members?"

"As well as I can. Keep in mind...I didn't always have this role. I was a member, too. But the couple that organized it split ways. Shortly before they separated, the wife asked me to take over. I was happy to do it."

"And what was her name?"

"Tanya Rose."

Mackenzie typed the name down on her note app on her phone. "So back to the HIV rumors," she said.

"Well, in the email I sent Devin O'Leary, I had asked if the rumors were true and all he replied with was...well, here...I'll just show you."

Alexa pulled out her phone, opened up her email client, and scrolled to a particular email. Mackenzie read it, thinking that each word of the brief exchange painted a picture for motive. Of course, the timelines might not line up exactly; they'd have to look into it.

In the email exchange, Alexa wrote: *"I'm hearing some terrible rumors about you and wanted to touch base with you before I confirm your attendance on the cruise. Of course if these rumors are true, I can't allow you to participate. I also hear that Janelle has left you as a result of the topic of these rumors. Could you please send along her contact information so I can get in touch with her as well?*

The response from Devin O'Leary came three days later, exactly six days ago. *"Rumors are none of your business. And no, you can't have Janelle's contact info. Fuck you and your slutty event."*

Mackenzie handed the phone back to Alexa. "Has he been a problem before?"

"No. Not at all. Which is why I assume the HIV rumor is true. The affair, too. It's been quite a shock."

"And do the others that planned on coming to the event know about the rumors?"

"Yes," Alexa said. "That's how I originally heard about it."

Mackenzie leaned over to Rodriguez and whispered into his ear. "Can you make a call to see what your guys at the precinct can do to pull records on Devin O'Leary?"

Rodriguez nodded. As he pulled his phone out to the make the call, Hudson reclined back in his chair, arching his back. "Okay, so here we go," he said.

All eyes turned to the color monitors installed within a wooden panel. Only three were in use, all showing the separate arms of the third floor hallway.

"Right here," Hudson said as people trickled in and out of the cameras, "we can see the Springses go into their room."

He pointed to a couple pulling two suitcases behind them. The hallway was filled with others that were filing into their own rooms. But as Jack Springs turned toward the door to room 341 and reached for his keycard, Mackenzie could see his face quite clearly. They all watched as Jack and Vanessa walked into the room, the door closing behind them.

Hudson then sped the footage up a bit, but not so fast as to miss if anyone entered the room. They watched for roughly two minutes as people came and went in a fast-forwarded motion. They never saw anyone leave or enter the Springses' room.

"We're now coming up on the call for the safety briefing," Hudson said. "The announcement was made over the ship's broadcast system at ten o'clock on the dot."

Here, the hallways were not as hectic. Only a few people milled around. The counter in the corner of the screen showed that the footage they were watching was recorded at 10 p.m. Within a few seconds, people started to come out of their rooms to attend the briefing. A great many of them were already dressed in bikinis and bathing suits.

As the foot traffic within the hallways started to thicken, Mackenzie spotted a single person walking against the flow of traffic. They were headed in the direction of room 341 and they walked with their head down. It was pretty clear that this person did not have any interest in making eye contact with anyone else. They all watched as this figure approached room 341 and knocked.

From the angle of the camera, it was evident that the person knocking on the door was male. But it was hard to see any real features in his face. He was wearing a backpack over his right shoulder and it appeared to not have much packed inside of it.

"Alexa," Mackenzie said, "I don't suppose you can tell from this angle if that happens to be Devin O'Leary, can you?"

Alexa squinted at the screen and, after a few moments, shook her head. "It's impossible to tell. It *could* be. Looks to be around the same height."

The door was answered. The man stood there for a moment and then was allowed in. After that, the door closed.

Hudson let the footage play at the heightened speed once again. Mackenzie kept her eyes on the counter at the bottom of the screen. When the door opened and the same man once again appeared in the screen, four minutes and nine seconds had passed. The man looked to the left, then to the right, and then walked to the end of the hallway. There, he took the elevator.

"Now, if we look at the single camera footage from the entrance and exits down below," Hudson said, "we see this same figure eighty seconds later, getting off of the boat."

They watched as the man showed up on the mentioned footage. He walked briskly, spoke to the two people manning the check-in and passenger service kiosks, and then exited the ship.

"Damn," Ellington said.

Mackenzie felt the same frustration. She had worked on the assumption that the suspect had managed to get off of the ship before it started its journey, but held a small hope that he had remained. Until now.

"Mr. Hudson, I need to speak with those two employees," she said, pointing to the two people the suspect had just spoken to.

"That's doable," Hudson said. "But they aren't on the ship. They only work out of the offices, I believe. Still, I can find out who was on the schedule and get you their information."

"Alexa, do you have an address for Devin O'Leary?" Mackenzie asked.

"No, sorry. Just a phone number and email address."

"It doesn't matter," Rodriguez said. "I can have someone at the station pull it for you within a few minutes."

"That'll work," Mackenzie said. She then turned to look at Alexa. "In any of the footage you saw, are you *sure* you can't pinpoint it as being Devin O'Leary?"

"Nothing concrete, no. Like I said…the build appears to be the same."

Mackenzie, Ellington, and Rodriguez shared an uncomfortable glance. "That's not enough to go on, is it?" Rodriguez asked.

"No, it's not enough to bring him in," Mackenzie said. "But I think it's more than enough to warrant waking him up very early in the morning."

"Want some of my men to head out with you?" Rodriguez asked.

"No," Mackenzie said, already heading for the door. "Just make sure we've got an open interrogation room."

She took her leave without giving so much as a single goodbye or thank you to Hudson, Alexa, and Rodriguez. Ellington caught up with her as she made her way to the ship's exit and gave her a curious look.

"You okay?" he asked.

"No," she said. "This guy is brave and crafty. And worse than that, I keep feeling like I'm going around in circles on this."

"No, we're making progress," Ellington said. "This Devin O'Leary guys seems like a legit lead. While we're on the way to grab him, I'll make some calls to see if he can be linked to Tidal Hills or DCM."

She nodded, once again feeling herself slip out of control just as she had while interrogating Samuel Netti. The elusiveness of this case—complete with a man who seemed to be coming and going as he pleased while killing his victims—bore too much similarity to her father's case. And she hated the fact that it was getting under her skin so easily.

They were back in their car at 1:40. Mackenzie was quiet and brooding when she got back behind the wheel. The late hour no longer bothered her. The idea of fatigue was far away from her mind now. All she could see were those freshly bloodstained sheets in the Springses' room and the looming figure at their door in the security footage.

She knew that they had not been able to see his face, but she still felt like the bastard had been smiling at her, taunting her and a history that continued to haunt her.

CHAPTER TWENTY

Devin O'Leary lived in a quaint little two-story house in the less ritzy part of Golden Beach. The neighborhood was dark and quiet as Mackenzie pulled her rental car up alongside the address that Rodriguez had texted her shortly after leaving the cruise ship. As she and Ellington started up O'Leary's sidewalk, she went over the other information that Rodriguez had sent her—information that the Miami PD had quickly and efficiently put together for her.

O'Leary didn't have much of a record at all. A few parking tickets and a drunk-and-disorderly from back in his college days. Other than that, he appeared to be clean.

Other than debaucherous involvement in a swinging club, Mackenzie thought as she and Ellington climbed up his porch steps.

She hammered on the door hard and then pressed the doorbell a few times. She could hear it chiming in the house, muted through the walls. She let ten seconds pass and then started up again.

From inside, she got an understandably cranky response. "Who the fuck is that? Janelle, is that you?"

That backs up the rumor about his wife leaving him, Mackenzie thought.

When Devin O'Leary opened the door, he went through a wide range of emotions in a handful of seconds. First there was anger, then confusion, then alarm. He studied them with clearly sleepy eyes, unable to form any words just yet.

"Are you Devin O'Leary?" Mackenzie asked.

"Yeah. Who the hell are you?"

"Agents White and Ellington with the FBI," she said. "I do apologize for the late hour, but there's an extremely pressing matter we feel you may be able to assist us with."

He was either still partly asleep or confused beyond words because all he could manage to get out were a few garbled stutters. Finally, he seemed to come around and asked: "What is this about?"

"We need to know where you were earlier tonight, specifically between the hours of eight and eleven," Ellington said.

"I was here."

"Doing what?" Mackenzie asked.

"Drinking my ass off, if you must know," O'Leary said.

"You got anyone that can prove it?"

"No, but I have a shitload of empty bottles in here. Look…what the hell is this? Did Janelle put you up to this?"

"That's your wife, right?" Mackenzie asked. "She left you?"

A wretched look passed across O'Leary's face. He looked like he might reach out and punch Mackenzie at any moment.

"She did," he said. "And why does that warrant two FBI creeps knocking on my door at two in the morning?"

"We're here for something very different," Mackenzie said. "Mr. O'Leary, do you know a couple by the name of Jack and Vanessa Springs?"

O'Leary's eyes wandered a bit and he nodded slowly. "Swinging. Seriously? Is that what this is about? It couldn't have waited until morning? I'm not stupid. Swinging is not illegal."

"No, but murder is," Mackenzie said. "The Springses were found dead in a bed on a cruise ship tonight. A cruise ship that I have it on good authority you were scheduled to be on."

"Yeah," he said absently, still apparently processing the news that the Springses were dead. "But that didn't quite work out."

"There are rumors going around," Mackenzie said.

"About my health."

Mackenzie only nodded to confirm. She could tell that he was processing a lot in that moment. He was tired, in shock, and, if he was to be believed, drunk.

"How well did you know the Springses?" Mackenzie asked.

He shook his head. "I'm not talking about this. Not right now. I can't. I had too much to drink, I've been dealt some shitty news recently, and I…damn. I just can't—"

And then something unexpected happened. Devin O'Leary started sobbing. He covered his face with his hands and sank to his knees. He leaned against the frame of the opened door and wailed.

"Just take me," he said through tears. "Take me in. I don't care. I just…I'm done. I can't do this. I fucked up. Bad…"

Mackenzie and Ellington shared a look over his head. Mackenzie gave Ellington a nod of acknowledgment, a look that said: *You cuff him.*

Ellington started to do exactly that as Mackenzie stepped past O'Leary and into his home. She heard Ellington behind her, trying to approach the odd scenario with as much professionalism and care as possible.

"Come on, Mr. O'Leary," he was saying. "Let's get you down to the station. We'll get you some coffee and sort this all out."

Mackenzie, meanwhile, walked further into O'Leary's house to see if his story checked out. In the kitchen, she found that eight empty beer bottles were piled on top of a close-to-overflowing trashcan. A shot glass sat on the edge of the sink. She sniffed at it and smelled whiskey.

She ventured into the bedroom and found a pair of jeans and a T-shirt balled up at the foot of the bed. She fished through the pockets of the jeans and found a handful of coins along with a crumpled receipt. It showed that O'Leary had been telling the truth. He'd purchased a case of beer at a local convenience store at 7:56 that afternoon. For him to have done that, gone to the ship, murdered two people, then get back home and get as drunk as he could…that was impossible.

But there's definitely something going on with him, she thought as she made her way back through his house. She closed the door behind her, thinking that the fact he had known the Springses was worth looking into anyway.

She joined Ellington out at the car as he was closing the rear passenger door. "Everything good in there?" he asked.

"Yeah," she said. "He's not our guy, but—"

"But yeah," Ellington said. "Something's going on with him."

They pulled away from the sidewalk with O'Leary still sobbing quietly in the back seat. As they made their way back to the precinct, Mackenzie started looking out in the direction of the sea. It was back there somewhere, but was hidden by the buildings and the night. Even the palm trees seemed menacing, like looming giants trying to stomp down on her as they carried Devin O'Leary to the station.

***

Maybe it had been listening to O'Leary weeping the entire way from his house to the precinct…or maybe it was just biology. Whatever it was, Mackenzie found that she could no longer fight off the tiredness. She felt fatigue speeding in on at her like a bullet as she sat down across from O'Leary in the interrogation room. Although she had been in this room less than seven hours after interrogating Samuel Netti, it seemed like a new foreign place.

"On your porch, you said you'd done something bad," Mackenzie said. "And then you seemed to just break. I know this is not a church and I am a far cry from a pastor or priest, but is there anything you want to tell us? If you keep it in, we'll just dig. You pretty much gave us plenty of reason to do so on your porch."

"It's fine," he said. He looked very sad but was no longer crying. His earlier outburst had worn him out. He looked hollow and exhausted.

She could tell that O'Leary was a beaten man. She supposed there was only so much a man could take. She couldn't imagine what it must be like to receive the news that you had a disease that could very well kill you.

"My wife and I have been swinging for years now. I was never into porno so when things started to get dry in the bedroom, we checked out swinging. I know it sounds dumb and backwards, but it helped. I don't know. Never cared about the psychology of it all. But last year, we swung with this couple and...I don't know. The wife and I sort of hit it off. We started to see each other regularly. A full-blown affair...different than the swinging, you know."

"And who was this other couple?" Mackenzie asked, wondering if it might be one of the four couples she'd recently seen deceased.

"The Bryants," he said. "I wish...man, I just wish things could have been different. It's just all a mess. I found out three months ago that I wasn't the only guy she was seeing on the side. And by then, I had already started to get sick. I got the diagnosis three weeks ago. I told my wife everything. HIV. Affair. Everything. I'm so scared I gave it to Janelle, you know? But...shit. I was so fucking scared, you know? Scared. Mad. So I—"

He started to lose it here and although Mackenzie was already sure she knew where he was going with it, her tendency to try to find the best in everyone fought against the concept. But the words he spoke next confirmed it all.

Through sobs, he went on. Mackenzie was currently alone in the room with him but she could pretty much feel the tension within the observation room as Ellington and Rodriguez listened in.

"I slept with two other women after I got the diagnosis. I was...like a monster. I wanted to spread it. It felt like justice...it felt like...like I was getting even with the whole world."

My God, Mackenzie thought.

She felt herself trembling with anger and something that felt like sadness.

She got up from her chair and suddenly found it next to impossible to look at Devin O'Leary. She made fists of her hands, tightening them as much as she could to suppress the trembling. She was swallowing down disgusting retorts and accusations that would be entirely unprofessional. She was tired, she was pissed off, and everything felt like it was slipping away.

You're going to have a panic attack if you don't get out of this room right now.

Without saying another word to him, Mackenzie walked out of the interrogation room as quickly as she could without letting on that she was bothered. She skipped the observation room altogether and headed down to the small office that she'd been working out of. She stood there in the darkness and took several deep breaths.

What the hell is wrong with people?

It was not the first time the question had occurred to her. Her occupation was primarily centered on that question. She thought of the man currently sitting in the interrogation room and wondered at what point of his life things might have started to go awry. Childhood? High school? College?

She heard footfalls behind her. She turned to see Ellington cautiously approaching her. He looked at her with more concern than he had ever shown before. It made her want to throw her arms around him, to have him hold her in silence until her body lagged from sleep.

"Mackenzie," he said, his voice soft. "What's going on?"

She made fists of her hands, not wanting him to see her trembling. "It's just been a lot," she said. "Harrison's mom dying, this fucking case…that creep upstairs. And this case. It's all just—"

"Too much."

She nodded. "Just give me a second. I'll be back up in a while. I needed to step away from O'Leary for a few minutes or I was going to snap."

"You need more than a few minutes," Ellington said. "I know one night together doesn't make me a Mackenzie White expert, but you need sleep. Or, at the very least, rest."

"You haven't had any, either," she pointed out.

"I had a very good night's sleep the night before I arrived here," he said. "And you've been at this for going on three days. Go back to the motel. Lay down and close your eyes. You have my word that I'll wake you up at eight."

She looked to her watch and saw that it had somehow gotten to be 3:05.

"Don't even think about it," he said. "O'Leary's a monster for sure, but he's not the killer. And he's not going to be able to link us to the killer. If we want a productive day tomorrow, you need some rest."

She nodded and said, "Fine. But call me at seven, not eight."

"Hard ass," he said.

She walked toward the door and passed by him. She wanted to kiss him but she also did not want to appear like the vulnerable damsel in distress that needed a man's touch whenever she was feeling out of sorts.

"We need the names of the women he slept with since contracting it," she said on her way out. "They have to be notified."

"Rodriguez is doing that right now," he said. He paused for a moment and then, choosing each word carefully, added: "Do you want me to come with you? Do you need someone there?"

The thought was a pleasant one, but she shook her head. "No thanks."

He nodded and watched her go.

It's okay to need someone, she thought to herself as she made her way through the halls and to the main lobby. *Why do you do that? Why do you refuse to seek help from other people?*

For a moment, she thought of her father's bloody bed, his final resting place before being lowered in the ground. She also thought of the absent mother who had not been there for her.

And there's my easy answer, she thought.

She stepped outside into the stillness of the early morning hours. She wasn't sure she had ever felt so lost in her life—and it had very little to do with the case.

She got into her car and as she cranked it to life, she stared out into the night. The killer was out there somewhere, occupying that same darkness.

In her mind's eye, she saw each crime scene and how the hands of one member would always be slightly touching the other in their staged poses. There was something there, but she could not quite grasp what it was. It remained in her mind as she headed to the motel but faded away as the lure of sleep grew stronger with the passing of each block.

CHAPTER TWENTY ONE

She blissfully collapsed in bed at 3:40. She kicked her shoes off and stripped down to her underwear but made it no further. Even the thought of getting into comfortable sleeping attire was too much to think about. She had just enough time to glance at the clock on the bedside table before she was asleep.

And, almost as quickly, she found herself pulled away in the tidal force of a dream.

She found herself standing in the bedroom of Josh and Julie Kurtz. The bed was stained in blood—even more blood than had been present at the actual scene. Now it was splattered all over the walls and carpet. Some of it even dripped down from the ceiling, collecting in new puddles on the floor.

Her father stood beside her. There was a hole in his head where a bullet had torn through and ended his life. He was looking at the scene with her as if it were perfectly normal—as if he also had an FBI ID in his pocket and had been on this case with her from the very start.

"Too much blood," he said. "It was very bad here."

His voice was robotic and very far away—like someone was speaking through him from a megaphone two houses over.

Her father then walked to the bed and crawled into it. In a darkly humorous way, he collapsed into the bloodstained sheets. "Is it easier for you this way?" he asked. "This is why you'll never escape the memory of me. Why are you so hung up on it?"

At that moment, a figure came stumbling out of the Kurtzes' bedroom closet. It was Vanessa Springs, dressed in her too-revealing bikini. Her stab wounds were there, having mutilated her chest and stomach. She approached Mackenzie with a sultry bit of swagger to her step. When she smiled at Mackenzie, a thin trail of blood seeped over her bottom lip. She placed one blood-streaked hand on Mackenzie's shoulder and her other hand slipped inside of her shredded bikini top. She withdrew a white square, matted with blood.

Mackenzie took it and was not at all surprised by what she saw.

It was a business card. **Barker Antiques.**

"Mackenzie," her father said from the bed. He was now pale and lifeless, exactly the way he had been when she had discovered him so many years ago as a young girl. "What the hell are you waiting for?"

He started to laugh, and Vanessa Springs followed his example. Blood came out of her mouth, pooling on the floor and on Mackenzie's feet.

She jerked awake, her heart hammering.

For a panicked moment, she looked down at the bed, half expecting to be on the bloodied bed of Josh and Julie Kurtz. But she was in her motel, taking a rest that Ellington had strongly suggested. It then occurred to her that her phone was ringing. She had not merely been torn from her sleep by the nightmare, but by the ringing of the phone.

As she reached for it, she saw on the clock on the table that it was 6:46.

"Hello?" she said, answering the call and trying not to sound as tired as she felt.

"Hey, Agent White," said a somber male voice. "It's Lee."

Hearing Harrison's voice was surreal. It made her wonder if she was still dreaming. Oddly, the first thing she could think to say was: "I told you…call me Mackenzie. None of the Agent White stuff."

"I know. Sorry. Look…I'm calling to thank you for handling things for me when I got the call about my mom."

"Sure," she said. "All I did was make some calls. How are you doing?"

"Fine, I think. I'm at my sister's house in Arlington. The funeral is tomorrow."

"With all due respect, you didn't have to call me at six forty-five in the morning to thank me," she said. "What's going on, Lee?"

"Well, I got a call last night from a contact I'd been using on the back end of things. Nothing official…sort of a shady go-to. McGrath okayed it. It was a guy I was using to see if I could get any clues about your father's case."

Now wide awake, Mackenzie sat up in bed. "And you didn't tell me?"

"I didn't. It was McGrath's orders and, quite frankly, I thought it was a good idea. No sense in you getting overly obsessed with the case when you aren't officially on it."

This irritated her to no end, but she knew it was the right thing to do. Still, she also could not help but feel like she had been left in the dark.

"So what did this guy want?" she asked, doing her best to move on.

"He says he thinks he might have a lead on an old business called Barker Antiques. It's been closed for years now. And even when it was open for business, it apparently didn't do well."

"Where was it out of?"

"New York. He's making some calls today to confirm and will get back to me. Look…I haven't even told McGrath about this yet. I figured I should bring it to you first. I'm telling you this part of it because as hard as it is going to be, *please* sit on this for a day or so. And if McGrath breaks the news to you, try to act surprised."

Already, the need to delve deeper into this was overwhelming. Especially after coming out of the nightmare she'd just had.

Priorities, she told herself. *Your first concern is to wrap this swingers case.*

"Yeah," she said. "I can do that."

"Okay. How's it going there anyway? I hear he sent Ellington to fill in for me."

"He did. It's going slower than I'd like but I think we're making some progress. As for you…let me know if I can do anything for you when I get back into town. Sorry again to hear about your mother."

They ended the call and she rolled out of bed. She peeled out of her underwear and took a quick shower. She was putting on the last of her clothes when a knock sounded at her door. She checked the time and saw that it was 7:20.

He's late, she thought with a smile. *On purpose, I'm sure, wanting to give me a few more minutes of sleep. If he only knew…*

She answered the door and found Ellington waiting on the other side. He somehow looked very much awake. He smiled at her and offered her one of the two coffees he held in his hands.

"Coffee is essential," he said. "It simply can't wait. Breakfast, though…I figured we could sit down somewhere and have that together. That sound like something you'd be up for?"

"Sounds great," she said.

But in the back of her head and heart, she wondered what Harrison's contact had found and what sort of links were tied to her business card in a long-forgotten business in New York.

CHAPTER TWENTY TWO

He woke up shortly after seven o'clock. As usual, he took a moment to himself before he got out of bed. Sometimes he simply needed to orient himself, to make sure he knew where he was and what had potentially happened the night before. He never drank, as it muddied his thoughts and actions, so the hangover haze he'd heard about wasn't an issue. No, for him it was something else. Something mental. Something he had been living with ever since he was a boy.

He felt a leg draped over his own. He looked to his right and saw a blonde woman, rather young. She was completely nude, sleeping on top of the covers, her body partially clinging to his. She was very pretty and had smudges of eyeliner on the side of her face. Slowly, the events of last night came to him. He was both satisfied and saddened by them.

He'd picked her up at a bar—the kind of place that sells two-dollar beers twice a week and has a ladies' night where watered down fruity liquor drinks are featured. She'd been an easier conquest than most other women. If he recalled, she'd said something about a boyfriend dumping her two days ago. Sensing her need for revenge, he'd spent the remainder of the night with her and had eventually come back to her place.

He wasn't sure if the sex had been good or not. He barely remembered it. Besides, in the same way she had been using him to get over an ex, he had been using her, too. He needed the sexual release if he was going to finish his work.

Thinking of the work, he gently pried her leg off of his body and slipped out of bed. He watched her sleep for a moment, making sure she was not going to rouse. She seemed dead to the world, taking deep breaths and oblivious of his movement.

He stepped out of her bedroom and quietly walked down the small hall until he found the bathroom. There, he cleaned himself up. He washed his face, washed himself from the waist down to rinse the activities of last night from him, used mouthwash, and splashed cold water into his face. He then returned to the bedroom, gathered his clothes, and headed out.

He left her apartment without her even knowing he had left. It was the second time he'd done such a thing in the last two weeks.

He'd done it numerous times ever since his wife had left. He knew it wasn't the typical way a newly single forty-year-old man should spend his life, but it was necessary.

He had been preparing himself for the murders for about three months now. And while there was no real sexual enticement in the murders themselves, it *did* cause a certain stirring of lust after the fact. And he had learned a long time ago that any form of lust caused him to grow distracted—violent, almost.

And that was odd to him because the very act of killing made him feel strangely at peace. He was not naïve enough to feel that there was a certain sort of justice being dealt out. Nor did he really think he was doing the world a favor. But it just made him feel like he had done something *right.*

He was still slightly thrumming with electricity from having killed the Springses on the cruise ship. It had been far too easy. Vanessa had opened the door to him, thinking that he was coming by for what Jack had referred to as a threesome warm-up for the night's events.

He'd killed them easy enough, getting Jack first because he was a huge son of a bitch. The element of surprise was eliminated when he busted in on Jack as he had started to unpack his things in the bathroom. He'd been a massive headache to get back in the bed to stage the scene.

But then, two hours later, he had been in that bar. Chatting with the blonde had seemed normal, felt good. The murders had been noting—just some strenuous exercise that he kept tucked in the back of his mind as he drew closer and closer to bedding the blonde.

When he reached the front steps of her apartment complex, he breathed in the morning air. He could smell the ocean and the exhaust of morning traffic.

It was a new day.

And it was a day where he fully planned to finish his work. He had one more couple he needed to…*meet with.* The meeting had already been arranged and as greedy as it seemed, he couldn't help but get a little turned on by it.

He'd saved the best for last. He held a special place in his heart for this last couple. The sight of the wife, naked and straddling him, had stuck in his mind for far too long. It had been one of the handful of reasons his marriage had ended.

But first, coffee. And then maybe he'd go home and get some work in.

He walked toward the nearest bus stop, his car still at the bar from last night. The sun was shining, the sky was an achingly beautiful blue, and the magic of Miami seemed to waver and dance all around him.

It was going to be a great day.
By the end of it, this last couple would be dead.
And finally, he would be free.

CHAPTER TWENTY THREE

Mackenzie was apparently hungrier than she thought. After putting down two cups of coffee, she ate two eggs, two sides of bacon, hash browns, and a bowl of oatmeal. Ellington, finishing up his southwester omelet, couldn't help but smile.

"How you keep your awesome figure is beyond me. I showed up late at night two nights ago and you had been scarfing down pizza. And now this breakfast...yeesh."

"A girl's gotta eat," she said.

"Did you get a good rest?" he asked.

She shrugged. "It was enough. How about you? You've been up for quite a while, too."

"I got a power nap between four thirty and six thirty. I'll be good until tonight. And hopefully by then, we'll have this thing wrapped up. Any ideas on your plate?"

She had a few but was hesitant to latch on to one because they all felt flimsy. "A few," she said. "I want to look into this woman Alexa mentioned...Tanya Rose. If she was part of the group Alexa is in charge of, maybe she'll know about any loose cannon sort of people we could be on the lookout for. How about you?"

"I'll probably pore over more paperwork and files down at the precinct. I can sic some officers on hunting down this Tanya Rose for you, too. Want to join me?"

"Not particularly," she said.

"You're the agent that needs to be out moving around to feel productive, right?" he said.

"Most of the time."

The table fell into silence for a moment as Mackenzie polished off her breakfast. Ellington sat forward, looking anxious.

"How are things going with the case out in Nebraska?" he asked. "With your dad and this newer victim?"

"The same," she said. She wasn't sure why she was keeping Harrison's newest revelation from him. For right now, it just seemed a little too personal. She also wasn't sure why she didn't feel comfortable with Ellington talking about her father's case.

Because it's none of his business, she thought. *Of course, it's just him trying to be sympathetic. He genuinely cares. Maybe he made the mistake of thinking that because you've now slept together, he can ask more personal questions.*

It was a sweet thought, but she wasn't ready to get into anything that deep with him yet. And it had nothing to do with him.

She didn't want to talk about her father's case with *anyone*. Especially now that there was a potential lead.

"You okay?" he asked.

"Yeah," she said. And then, assuming he'd be able to handle the blunt truth, she added: "My dad's case isn't something I like to talk about."

"I get that. But you have to talk to *someone* about it, right? I mean, you've got that detective back in Nebraska keeping an eye out, right?"

She honestly hadn't even thought of Kirk Peterson in a while— not until Harrison had called her this morning. It made her want to call Peterson right then and there to get more details. But again, she was distracted by how much Ellington knew about her father's case.

"How do you know so much about the case?" she asked.

He shrugged but an uncomfortable look touched his face. He sensed that he had stepped into dangerous territory but it might be too late to step back. "When I took an interest in you, I took an interest in that case."

"But I've never really talked to you about it," she said.

"I know. But I wanted to…hell, Mackenzie. I wanted to know more about you. And not just for some selfish ambition. You're a great agent. I knew you'd be a great agent from the first time I saw you; that's why I recommended you try for Quantico in the first place. Besides…you did talk to me about it once, in passing. Back in Nebraska when I was sent out there to help with the Scarecrow Killer. Remember?"

She honestly didn't remember mentioning it to him. But she had been so enamored and overwhelmed by his presence back then that it was all an embarrassing recollection. She had tried so hard to put that first meeting with Ellington out of her mind that it was all really just a blur to her.

"And you did what?" she asked, knowing there was a flare of anger in her voice but not caring. "Just thought you'd dig around and find out more about me and my past?"

"Um…no. But I did look into the case file just to familiarize myself with it. Is that so bad?"

"No, it's not bad. It's just…that's very personal to me."

He held up his hands in mock surrender—and for some reason, that offended her more than anything else. "Fine," he said. "Sorry. It won't happen again."

"It's not something to be so flippant about," she said. She felt a tremor in her voice but wasn't sure if it was the result of looming anger or sorrow.

"I'm not being flippant about anything," he said. "Look, seriously, I'm sorry. I didn't know this was such a big deal. And I—"

"Of course it's a big deal," Mackenzie said. She felt anger rising up in her like an angry hive of hornets and, honestly, she had no real idea where it was coming from. Sure, she felt slightly betrayed but underneath all of that, she knew she was overreacting. Maybe she was just too tired, or maybe she was too worked up about this case.

"Jared, I know you mean well, but please shut up."

She couldn't remember if she had ever used his first name to his face before. It felt monumental in a weird way. It felt intimate.

"Shut up, huh?" he said, clearly pissed.

"Yes. Just—"

Ellington stood up, not even looking at her. "I'm going to catch a cab back to the precinct and get to work. Maybe come by and say hi when you're not being so irrational."

She almost spoke up and asked him to stay. But she bit the words back, not wanting to seem too desperate. She watched him walk away and stared into her now-empty mug of coffee.

Great, she thought. *Just what I need: relationship drama in the middle of this hopeless case. How the hell did I even get here? How did this happen?*

The waitress came by and refilled her cup. Mackenzie sipped at it slowly, staring off into space and trying her best to sort through the names, events, and crime scenes in her head. With a mind still wanting more sleep, it was surprisingly easy to focus on singular trains of thought. It slowed down her usually frantic pace.

With Samuel now out of the picture and useless, and Gloria and DCM apparently a dead end, what does that leave me? For starters, it leaves me with a sick feeling for Miami—the knowledge that these seedy little sex clubs are thriving so well. How in God's name am I supposed to find a single link between all of the victims? If these things are so isolated that they head out to sea on cruises, how can I pin anything down?

She thought about the cruise ship, of seeing that bit of footage. The killer had entered and then left the Springses' room. She'd been sure that had been the last thing they'd need to wrap the case. But no...here she was, as clueless as ever.

Maybe the excitement of seeing the killer on the screen left some loose ends, she thought. *There's more there, details about the cruise and the swingers' event that went untouched.*

She knew this was right and felt irresponsible for leaving so many things unturned. Quickly downing her third cup of coffee, she opened up the notes app on her phone and pulled up the notes she'd taken last night as she and Ellington left the cruise ship.

She had taken down Alexa's phone number with Alexa giving an enthusiastic promise to help in any way she could. Just like Gloria at DCM, Alexa seemed to have been genuinely shocked and disgusted that someone she might have been involved with in a business sense was killing people.

Mackenzie punched the number in and the line was answered after three rings.

"Hello?" Alexa said, her voice ragged and tired.

"Alexa, it's Mackenzie White. Do you have a moment?"

There was a slight jostling of the phone from the other end. Although it was after eight o'clock in the morning, it was clear that Alexa was still in bed. It made sense, as she probably ended up getting to bed later than Mackenzie had the night before.

"Yeah. What's up?"

"I was hoping to ask you a few more questions about the event that had been planned for last night."

"I guess I could do that," she said. "I'm pretty sure the ship ended up leaving this morning, though. I don't know how many people going to the event stayed on."

"That's fine," Mackenzie said. "I just have some basic questions."

"Okay. Do you think you could ask them over breakfast?"

Mackenzie looked down at her empty plate and cup with a smirk. "Yeah, I can do that. Where and when can you meet me?"

"Give me an hour, please," Alexa said. She then gave Mackenzie a meeting place and the women ended the call.

When Mackenzie headed out for her car, less than ten minutes had passed since Ellington had left. She thought about calling him to let him know where she was headed. But if he was anything like her, he'd probably need some time to cool down.

If anything comes out of this meeting with Alexa, I'll call him right away.

She started the car and pulled out into morning traffic. She was tired, she was at a loss in terms of the case, and if she had any more coffee, she was going to get the jitters. If she didn't find some huge revelation between now and the early afternoon, she was going to *have to* get some rest—more than just a handful of hours this time.

As she drove onward, a beautiful Miami morning unspooled before her. She barely noticed it, though. Her mind was wrapped around this case so tightly now that even the recent news about her father's case was momentarily dwarfed. She headed for her meeting with Alexa, feeling the gorgeous seaside sun through the windshield but barely registering it at all.

CHAPTER TWENTY FOUR

She found herself in yet another greasy-spoon diner forty minutes later. She opted for water rather than coffee and, surprised to find that she was still a bit hungry, ordered a fruit and yogurt parfait, hoping the natural sugars of the fruit would give her a bit of an energy boost.

Alexa had not really done much preparation to herself before coming out. She wore a pair of clingy jogging pants and a long-sleeved shirt. Her hair was in a messy ponytail and she wore no makeup. She was still very pretty and Mackenzie found it odd that a woman of her appearance would be involved in something like an underground swinger and sex club.

"I know what you think of me," Alexa said, as if reading Mackenzie's mind.

"What do you mean?"

"I get it all the time," Alexa said. "Especially from some of my closer friends that know what I do. I'm thirty-four and have a body a twenty-one-year-old would kill for. I don't say that to be conceited—I've worked my ass off for this body. But the general consensus is that because I'm a woman approaching forty, I should be thinking about getting a husband and popping out a kid."

It wasn't *quite* what Mackenzie had thought, but it was close. She only nodded in response.

Alexa shrugged. "I don't have any reasons for it. Honestly, I'm not even one of those women that *has* to have sex. I've seen those women before and I know some of them are messed up. Some feel like they need it because of abuse from their past—they think it's all they are good for. I've also seen women come along to these clubs because they so badly want to please their husbands. But me...I don't know. I like the energy. And sure...when I *am* in the mood for it, it's nice. It makes you feel wanted...desired."

"With all due respect," Mackenzie said, "I did not call you to ask you to justify your need for being in a club like this."

"Oh, I know. It's just that after last night, I think I understand the stigma about these types of things a bit better. Unless you really know the people you're getting involved with, these things can be very dangerous. There's a level of trust there, and I think it's missing from these events most of the time."

"Speaking of that level of trust," she said, "I'd like to know more about the Springses. Was this the first time you'd seen them?"

"No. There are a few regulars that pop up at most of these events, and they were one of them."

"How about the Kurtzes, Carlsons, and Sterlings? Do those last names ring any bells?"

Slowly, almost as if operated by a rusted spring, Alexa nodded. Realization dawned in her eyes as she started to understand what this could mean.

"How did you know them?" Mackenzie asked, sensing that a huge connection might be within her grasp.

"The Sterlings came to two of the events I put on," she said. "The Kurtzes came to one. As for the Carlsons, I believe they signed up for one but never showed up. But if they signed up for one of my events, I can pretty much guarantee you that they were involved in other swinging events or sex clubs."

More than you know, Mackenzie thought.

Apparently, she was too tired to maintain much of a poker face. Alexa's face went slightly pale and her eyes narrowed in concern. "Are they…have they all been killed?"

"They have," Mackenzie said. "And up until now, you are the only resource I have that can connect every single one of the victims. So please…think very hard about this. Can you think of any couple that was involved in any capacity with all four of these couples?"

Alexa stared at her breakfast, only partially eaten. The shock and surprise was still on her face, but she nodded. "I can think of two right away. But one of them moved away about seven or eight months ago. Atlanta, I think. But the other one…yeah, I know them pretty well. They divorced not too long ago."

Swinging apparently doesn't work as well as some seem to think, Mackenzie thought. *Seems to be a lot of divorce…*

"I need a name," Mackenzie said.

"The Fallens," she said. "Mark and Ellie. I don't know if they were involved with all four of the couples, but I know for sure they can be connected to the Springses and the Carlsons."

"Do you have any idea why the Fallens divorced?" Mackenzie asked.

"Not for sure, no. Word on the street is that Ellie met some other guy and preferred him over her husband."

"Do you know if this other guy she met was part of any clubs?"

"No idea. But if I recall, the Fallens were good friends with the Springses. I'm pretty sure they did some other events and clubs together. They were sort of…well, they were sort of an item for a while. All four of them."

"Mark and Ellie Fallen," Mackenzie said, committing it to memory.

"Yes."

"And what can you tell me about Tanya Rose? If she used to run this little club, do you think she'd know more than you about some of the members?"

"I don't know," Alexa said. "Probably not. At the risk of sounding dramatic, she was sort of a bitch. I doubt she even remembers the names of any of the members. After she and her husband divorced, she moved to California or something with the guy she was sleeping with."

"What about the husband? Did you know him?"

"Not well. I met him a few times. Seemed like an okay guy. Just always in her shadow."

"I don't suppose you have their contact information, do you?"

"I have an email for Tanya, but the last thing I sent to it came back to me as undelivered. I guess she killed the account. She really wanted to distance herself from the swinging stuff, you know?"

Mackenzie slid out of the booth seat and got to her feet. "I hate to leave you alone to finish up your breakfast," Mackenzie said, "but I need to get going."

"Sure. And best of luck. Please let me know if there's anything else I can do to help."

"I may just have to do that. Thanks again."

Mackenzie paid for her minuscule meal and then walked quickly out of the diner. Before she made it to her car, she pulled out her cell phone again. This time, she dialed up Gloria with DCM.

"Hello?" Gloria said. She sounded on edge, as if she had been expecting just about any call coming in ever since Mackenzie and Harrison had spoken with her to present bad news.

"Gloria, it's Mackenzie White. Listen…I got another name of a couple that's involved in swinging. I know you vehemently didn't want to hand out a list of every single member, but I need to see if this name is on your member list. And at the risk of sounding like I'm threatening you, I'm going to need you to comply. If you don't, I can make things very difficult for you. I hate to play that card, but that's where we're at right now."

Gloria didn't even hesitate, though she did sound irritated when she responded. "What's the name?"

"Mark and Ellie Fallen."

"Yeah, I know that name. I don't think they've been active in a while, though. I can check my records to confirm that."

"No need," Mackenzie said, assuming Gloria didn't know that the Fallens had divorced. "Do you know right offhand any couples that the Fallens might have been involved with?"

"Well, they were very tight with the Springses," Gloria said. "And I think they at least spoke with the Kurtzes, though I don't ever recall them hooking up. If they did, it was on their own time."

"Thanks," Mackenzie said.

She heard Gloria start to say something else, but Mackenzie killed the call. She got into her car and pulled up yet another number. She nearly pushed Ellington's name but wasn't quite ready for that yet. Besides, she didn't want to use him as an errand boy. Instead, she called up Officer Dagney.

Dagney answered on the second ring. She sounded far too bright and cheerful for Mackenzie's taste. "Agent White," she said. "What can I do for you?"

"I need an address and contact information for Mark and Ellie Fallen. The sooner the better."

"I'll have it texted to you within five minutes."

Once again, Mackenzie got back out on the road. Not having Ellington in the passenger seat was refreshing for a moment. It allowed her to not have to pretend to be vigorously energized. She was tired as hell and without anyone riding passenger, she could show it.

Her cell phone dinged two minutes later as a text came in. It was Dagney, working quickly as usual. Mackenzie inserted the Fallens' address into her GPS and then called the number for Mark Fallen.

It was nearing ten o'clock in the morning and the day already felt excruciatingly long. But with a solid lead that connected each of the murdered couples, Mackenzie started to feel the itch of progress as her body fought off her sluggishness and found its second wind.

CHAPTER TWENTY FIVE

Over the next couple of minutes, Mackenzie spoke to both Mark and Ellie Fallen while traveling to the address Dagney had sent her. While neither of them had seemed overly anxious to speak with her, Mackenzie was able to piece together bits and pieces of the last few months of the Fallens' lives.

She spoke to Ellie first. She had been at work and, as a result, had seemed rushed. Even after Mackenzie had identified herself as working for the FBI, Ellie Fallen (still having not gone through the paperwork of changing her last name) was resistant.

"I'm at work and really don't have time for this," she spat.

"I understand that," Mackenzie said. "But what's going to be easier? Answering a few questions over the phone or having me come to your work and hassle you there?"

"That would be rude and impossible," Ellie said. "I moved to Jacksonville after the divorce," she said. "You say you're on assignment in Miami…and that's one hell of a drive."

"Ms. Fallen, in the time you've spent pissing and moaning with me, you could have already answered my questions."

"Jesus. Fine. What do you want?"

"I want to know about your relationship with Jack and Vanessa Springs. I'd also like to know about your history with any events you and your former husband attended that were organized by a woman named Alexa."

"You've got to be kidding me," Ellie said.

"No, I'm not. I fear someone you and your former husband might have been involved with has been killing couples involved in the swinging community."

"Well, you'll have to talk to Mark about that," Ellie said. "That's not a part of my life anymore."

"Yes, but—"

With that, Ellie Fallen hung up. Now halfway to the Fallen residence, Mackenzie dialed up Mark Fallen. He answered pretty much right away and sounded rather chipper. In the background, Mackenzie could hear faint music.

"Hello?"

"Mr. Fallen? This is Mackenzie White, an agent with the FBI."

"FBI?"

"That's correct."

She waited a second as the music in the background came to a stop. "Sorry, one second…okay, so…FBI?" he asked again. "Um, what can I do for you?"

"Mr. Fallen, are you at home by any chance?"

"I am. I work from home."

"Good. I need to speak with you about a pending investigation. I'll be there in fifteen minutes."

***

Mark Fallen was clearly living the life of a recently divorced man. The house wasn't necessarily in a shambles, but it certainly hadn't been properly cleaned in quite some time. There were empty soda cans and papers scattered all along the coffee table in the living room. Mark tried his best to lead Mackenzie quickly through the mess and into his office. His office wasn't in much better shape than the living room, but it at least held some degree to professionalism. From the posters and art on the walls, she assumed he was some sort of graphic designer.

"Mr. Fallen, this shouldn't take long," Mackenzie said, taking a seat in a chair on the opposite side of the office from his desk. "And I certainly hope you'll be more help than your wife was on the phone."

"Well, I can almost guarantee that," he said. "Seeing as how she decided to morph into this monstrous raging bitch. What's going on?"

"Well, a string of murders has led the FBI into a search of what could be considered underground clubs. Swingers' clubs and things like that."

"Say no more," Mark said. "Guilty as charged. Ellie and I tried it out to see if it might create a spark in a dry marriage. It did for a while, but…anyway, I digress. What can I do to help?"

"Well, you and your wife seem to have had some sort of involvement with everyone that has been murdered so far. We have spoken with three different venues that engage in swinging and so far, this is the only solid match we have."

"Oh my God," Mark said. "Can I…can I ask which couples?"

She told him the names of the four couples and he seemed legitimately shocked. "And these…these are *recent*?"

"All within the last eight days," Mackenzie said.

"Jack and Vanessa?" he asked, clearly near tears. "You're *sure*?"

"Yes."

"My God. Did you...did you tell Ellie when you spoke with her?"

"No. She didn't really give me the chance. Now, Mr. Fallen...while we can't tag you and your former wife as suspects just yet—nor do I want to—I *can't* overlook the fact that you've been connected with all of them. So I need you to think back to any interactions you had with these couples. Can you think of any other link? Any other way they might all be connected?"

Mark Fallen reclined somberly in his desk chair. His eyes rolled from side to side as he thought about it. Slowly, he sat up and started to habitually bite at his lower lip.

"I don't know if it would be important or not," he said. "But the first time Ellie and I were with the Springses, we also haphazardly met the Sterlings. It was at DCM. They were sort of laughing nervously about this guy that had tried to talk his way into a group thing. A couples thing, you know? Most of the time, there are individuals connected with swingers' clubs just because some couples like to have just one more body in there...you know? Anyway...they were saying this guy sort of spazzed out and got all weepy and depressed when they told him they weren't interested. And that made Ellie and I recall the same sort of thing a few months before that, at another event."

"Was there a connection there?" Mackenzie asked.

"We never found out for certain," Mark said. "But we gave a description of the guy and it seemed to fit what the Sterlings were talking about."

"Were you part of a club when you met the Sterlings and discussed this man?"

"Yeah, it was with DCM. Our first time there."

"How long did you guys stay with DCM?"

"Not long," Mark answered. After we tried swinging through Alexa's events a few times, we sort of decided it wasn't for us. DCM was our last go of it. Even when we made fast friends with the Springses, it never really worked. It was exciting and all, but...not really for us."

"You said you thought the man the Sterlings had been discussing reminded you of a man at another event. What event was that?"

"There was one really weird story from an event at a hotel two years or so ago. Ellie and I were at the event with the Springses. It's not one of my prouder moments but...things got out of hand. There were four of us...four couples at the same time. The Kurtzes were one of them. So you've got the Springses, the Kurtzes, then Ellie

123

and I. And then the fourth couple. Things had just started getting heated and the guy…he sort of loses his shit, you know. Starts getting mad. I'm not trying to be funny here, but he couldn't get it up. He was absolutely livid. And as he got mad, he still kept trying to be part of it all, you know? But even his wife didn't want him near her. He ended up getting thrown out."

"How?" she asked. "Security?"

"No, there really wasn't much security at those kinds of things. No…Jack punched him and then some other guy hauled him out. I even remember Ellie trying to stop all the fighting. When Jack knocked the guy out, she was there on the floor with him. She was the only one that tried to help him."

"Do you remember the name of the other guy?"

"No."

"Do you recall anyone else that was at the event?"

"I know faces, I guess. But not names."

"Okay…so we've verified that you knew the Springses, the Sterlings, and the Kurtzes. Did you ever meet the Carlsons?"

"If I did, they're not sticking out in my head."

Mackenzie pulled out her phone, opened a PDF of the case file, and opened up the .jpeg of the Carlsons. It was from Toni Carlson's Facebook page. She showed it to Mark and watched as recognition bloomed over his face.

"Yeah. That's one of the guys that hauled him out."

And now all the dots connect, Mackenzie thought. *This guy was in the same group with the Kurtzes and the Springses for sure. Then Stephen Carlson escorted him from the building after he got angry. And he's likely the same deranged guy the Sterlings were talking about when the Fallens first met them. He's been connected to all of the dead couples.*

Then why not Mark and Ellie Fallen? she wondered.

Mark just said that Ellie was the only one that tried to help him. Maybe he saw that as an act of kindness and left them off of his kill list.

"Are you sure you don't remember the man's name?" Mackenzie asked.

"No. I'm sorry. I was about to say that I think Alexa might know it, but this was right after she took over. She was at the event but I don't even think she saw any of it."

"How about any other couples he might have been involved with?"

124

Mark shrugged. "I don't know for sure. But I'm pretty sure he and his wife swung with this one couple a few times—the Vaughans."

"You're sure of that?"

"Yeah."

"Was it through Alexa or DCM?"

"DCM, I think. This guy never showed up to Alexa's events again."

Mackenzie started to connect the dots in her head. She now had a potential lead on the killer (assuming Alexa had a name) as well as another couple that could be in serious danger. It felt like a very dangerous equation, but at least she was getting somewhere now.

"Thank you very much for your time," she said, standing and moving instantly for the door.

"This is terrible," Mark said, following slowly behind her. "Do you think the Vaughans are in trouble?"

Almost definitely, she thought.

But what she said was: "I don't know. But if they are, I think your willingness to answer my questions might keep them safe."

She left his house feeling like she might have lied to him, but more determined than ever to make sure she had told him the truth.

Marching back to her car, she called Alexa once again. This time, Alexa answered on the first ring and did not sound tired at all.

"Hi, Agent White. Any news?"

"Maybe," she said. "I just spoke with Mark Fallen. He told me an account from an event you held in a hotel two years ago. There was some sort of altercation and—"

"Yes, I remember. That was my first official event. If you want to call it that. I think Jack Springs lost his temper and hit someone."

"Mark tells it a little differently. He says this guy got really mad. He was having sexual problems and got really upset. Started freaking people out. Do you remember the name of this guy?"

Alexa was quiet for a moment, apparently realizing what this could mean. She then gave Mackenzie a name and when she did, even her tone of voice indicated that they had likely stumbled upon the identity of the killer.

CHAPTER TWENTY SIX

Byron Decker watched the couple from behind the wheel of his small-bodied pickup truck. He'd been watching them for a while, really. Three months, in fact.

Damn, he thought. *Has it really been three months?*

This couple was the last. This would be the end of his work. Finally, he would be able to live his life free of the ridicule and pain that had shadowed him for the past two years.

While he had indeed been watching them for three months, Decker still wasn't exactly sure what they did for work. Whenever the man left the house, he was dressed in either a nice suit, complete with a tie, or mesh shorts and a tank top for his morning and afternoon runs (depending on the day of the week). And when the woman left the house, she was normally dressed in casual attire. Neither of them came and went with any regularity, making Decker think they either both worked from home or the man did some sort of banking or trading nonsense—something that caused him to dress nice from time to time, but also allowed him to come and go as he pleased, at whatever hours best suited him.

This couple had been tricky to pinpoint. With the other couples, there had at least been some regularity to their schedules. After a few weeks, he'd been able to strike with confidence. But this couple…they were liked flies. They buzzed around whenever they wanted. Last month they had left for nine days straight, apparently on some sort of vacation if the suitcases they'd carried out behind them were any indication.

They'd both come out together earlier today. They'd left in their expensive car and then come back home three hours later. Now, shortly before noon, they were pottering around in the front yard, trimming up the landscaping. It was such a domesticated thing to do—both pretentious and cute all at the same time. The husband was carrying bags of mulch while the woman was trimming weeds out of the large flower beds. She was dressed in such a way that made him think she either wasn't sure how to dress for yard work or simply didn't care if she got her cutesy tight little clothes dirty.

He'd seen them before, of course. He'd seen them naked, at their most vulnerable. And seeing them now, perfectly happy and tending to their stupid lawn, infuriated him.

I could kill them right now, he thought. *I could walk by like any pedestrian or loser out walking. And it would be over.*

As tempting as it was, he knew he had to keep his cool. He'd been waiting for this to end for nearly two years now—first summoning the courage and then spending this last week going to each of the couples and killing them. To ruin it now would mean everything else he had done would be fruitless…meaningless.

Besides…this was the last house, the last couple. He was parked two blocks down, watching them. For the last few months, he had been dividing his time between the five different houses, watching the couples come and go. He'd learned their schedules and, in some cases, had even watched to see where the spare key was hidden.

In the end, he had relied on good old human kindness to get inside. He had knocked on the doors he had not been able to get the keys to. They had all recognized his face at once. The Kurtzes and the Carlsons had nearly shut the door in his face. But his pleas to simply let him speak, to hear him out, had won them over. He had given fake apologies for his behavior two years ago in the hotel. The only kink in the plan had been the Springses. He'd nearly been unable to get onboard the ship and ended up dropping two grand to get a ticket—which was refunded when he faked sick and claimed to no longer be able to make the trip.

He figured that might end up getting him in trouble—a surefire red flag for the cops to pursue sometime in the very near future. But by then, he planned on being in Mexico. An old lover of his lived in Juarez and had a nice little place where he could get drunk on Mexican beer every day.

But first, this couple. The Vaughans.

He'd move in tonight. Since they were the last couple, he wouldn't have to be as careful. Sure, he'd still stage them and posture them like the others. But if he was a little messier than usual, that would be okay. The moment he was done with them, he was going to be gone. By the time the police had the chance to figure out what had happened, he'd be crossing the border.

It made him want to act now. With the others, he'd waited until he was pretty sure they were nearly in bed. Or, in the case of the Sterlings, a few moments after he knew they'd turned the lights out and gone to bed.

But with the Vaughans, he wasn't sure he could wait until then. The neighborhood was mostly quiet. If he acted quickly, no one would even see him. He'd blend right in to the neighborhood. There was nothing suspicious about him, nor anything about his appearance that stood out.

Do it, he thought. *Just do it now and be done with it.*

God, it was tempting.

But he had to at least wait until they were inside. He couldn't very well kill them out in their yard, in plain daylight.

Fine, he thought. *I've waited nearly two years. I even lost a wife to this little crusade. I can wait a few more hours.*

So that's what he did.

Byron Decker sat in his pickup, gripping the wheel tight in his hands, waiting for the right moment to strike and end his killing spree.

CHAPTER TWENTY SEVEN

Mackenzie could barely even remember being exhausted earlier in the morning. Ellington making the wise demand that she get some rest very late at night was a distant memory. Because as she headed back for the precinct and called Ellington, she was suddenly wired. She felt this case coming to a close. More than that, she felt time pushing against her like a tide as she did everything she could to ensure that a fifth couple was not killed.

Ellington's voice chimed in her ear as he answered the phone. "Hey," he said. His voice was neither dry nor cheerful. He was clearly still upset but getting over it.

"I spoke to Alexa again this morning," she said. "She told me about another couple that was connected to all of the murdered couples. I just finished speaking with the husband and he told me about this guy…a very angry man that was also connected to all of the dead couples. A guy that was ridiculed and maybe even humiliated. And he just happens to be the ex-husband of the woman that ran the swinging club before Alexa took over."

There was a long pause.

"Do you have a name for this guy?"

"Byron Decker. I also got the name of a fifth couple that is directly related to this guy and his issues. Someone needs to find them to keep an eye out. I don't have first names."

"One second," he said. "Rodriguez is right here. I'm putting you on speaker. So it sounds like we need to get an address for this Byron Decker and then search for this couple. You got a last name?"

"Vaughan. I guess we can run through the member lists from DCM, Tidal Hills, and Alexa's list. It shouldn't take long."

"Sounds good," Ellington said. "You coming back here while we churn all this stuff together?"

"Yeah. I'm about half an hour away."

She ended the call, finding that she was quite glad that she'd be back in Ellington's company soon. It was more than just partnering with him and having him ride shotgun as they hopefully brought this case to a close. It was because she knew she worked better with him. She knew that her logic seemed to be sharper and she was always trying to do her absolute best. Not that she didn't feel at her best on her own; it was just better to be her best with Ellington.

She merged onto the interstate and raised her speed to ninety. The thrill of the hunt pushed her on. The bright blue Miami sky suddenly seemed vibrant and full of promise. And while she could not hear the sea from where she was, she could sense it in the distance, wide and endless, the waves crashing along the shore as if urging her on.

***

There was a stirring of excitement in the precinct when Mackenzie sprinted inside. Rodriguez, Dagney, and Nestler were gearing up and going over the details of the next few hours. She admired the way they worked—a well-oiled machine, making sure every cog was in its right place. Ellington stood with them and when he set his eyes on Mackenzie, he gave her a smile.

"We got addresses?" Mackenzie asked.

"We got one for Byron Decker," Rodriguez said. "We're still working on getting the names and address for a Vaughan couple tied to DCM or Tidal Hills."

"Good, let's get going."

"One second," Ellington said. "Come with me really quickly, would you?" He looked very serious as he took her by the arm and led her down the hall.

"Yeah. What is it?"

He held up a finger, telling her to wait a moment, as they hurried to the small conference room. He ushered her inside and closed the door behind them. He turned to her, saying nothing, and kissed her.

Frustration tried its best to rear its head. *What the hell is he doing? We're in a hurry and there's no time for this.*

But her heart and body gave in. She sank into the kiss and returned it. It was a brief one that was broken after about five seconds. When he stepped back, he sighed and smiled at her again. "Sorry," he said. "I had to. This morning…yeah, I maybe pushed too hard and—"

"And I was being a bitch. We were both in the wrong there. Water under the bridge."

"Good," he said. "Now, let's get to work."

They filed back out into the hallway and joined the three officers at the front of the building.

Mackenzie looked to Rodriguez as Nestler and Dagney flanked him to either side. "Rodriguez, you have the address, so you lead us there. But when we get to the address, Ellington and I will take the lead. When we get there, you guys don't even get out of your car until you see us going inside—that's whether things go smooth and easy or difficult. Got it?"

"Loud and clear," Rodriguez said.

The five of them exited the station and headed to their cars. As Mackenzie drove behind Rodriguez, she filled Ellington in on her morning. As she recounted it all, it made her again wonder how women like Gloria and Alexa had never thought to mention Byron Decker and his actions. Had it been willful negligence on their parts or had they both genuinely assumed he was not any sort of risk?

I can see the reasoning, I suppose, she thought. *A man with impotency issues that was embarrassed in a swinger setting would likely not want to show his face again. Makes him less of a threat.*

Behind all of that, there was yet another thought: *Don't get too cocky. While there are clear and evident links to this guy, there's no guarantee he's the killer.*

She tried to keep this reality in mind but something about this lead seemed solid. In the academy, she had heard about a certain feeling agents often got while in the field—feelings that they were onto something, or perhaps riding directly into a successful arrest…or potential danger.

She was feeling that now. And with Ellington being back beside her and making her feel a little more complete than she had felt earlier in the day, she felt that she had unstoppable momentum on her side.

It took nineteen minutes to reach the residence of Byron Decker. It was a modest little one-story saltbox in a lower-middle-class neighborhood. The yard looked well maintained and the porch was clean. A few hanging green plants hung from the corners, close to dying but still vibrant. The house did not have an accompanying garage, and there were no vehicles parked in front of the house or in the small concrete driveway.

She and Ellington slowly walked up to the small porch. If she needed any further confirmation that she did indeed feel like things were coming to a close, it came when she instinctually placed her right hand on the butt of her Glock, holstered at her side. She touched it lightly as they climbed the stairs.

She glanced behind them and saw that Rodriguez and his crew had done as instructed; they remained in their car, watching as Mackenzie and Ellington approached the front door.

Ellington knocked on the door. They were met with only silence from the other side. Ellington knocked again and shook his head.

"Pretty clear he's not home," he said.

Mackenzie thought things over, wondering what the best approach might be. The neighborhood was quiet and dead, paralyzed by the absence of people in the middle of the day.

We technically need a warrant, she thought. *While signs might be pointing to him, there's nothing concrete just yet.*

But if he is *the killer and we wait to get everything in order...there's one more couple. Maybe more. He could easily kill again—his quick turnaround time is evidence of that.*

Ellington could tell that she was thinking hard about it. "Your call," he said.

She nearly asked him to kick the door down. But she was making the decision and did not want him held responsible if they were reprimanded for it later.

She gave him a quick nod, drew her Glock, and took a single step back. She lunged forward and brought her leg up fast and hard. It connected squarely below the knob, right at the edge. She could not deny the surge of satisfaction that raced through her when the door swung open to the sound of splintered wood as the frame buckled and cracked.

She only caught a glimpse of Ellington's impressed expression as she walked inside. She was vaguely aware of the sound of car doors opening and closing behind her as Rodriguez, Dagney, and Nestler exited their car and came across the lawn.

Inside, the place was just as tidy as the porch. The front door led directly to a small living room, which was decked out in a nice television and a small corner that served as a study of sorts. A small sitting area separated the living room from the kitchen and the hallway that ran off of the kitchen and into the remainder of the house.

She and Ellington slowly staked out the house. They came to the house's only full bathroom, then the master bedroom and a guest bedroom. At first glance, there was nothing at all suspicious. Decker seemed to live a neat and organized life. He had a decent wardrobe hanging in his closet, and the appliances in the kitchen were all brand name and clean.

"No one's home," Mackenzie said as they cleared the final room.

"That makes our forced entry a little sticky then," Ellington commented.

Hearing Rodriguez and his partners quietly walking down the hallway, Mackenzie entered the hallway and shook her head. "We're clear."

Nestler and Dagney were unable to hide their disappointment, though Rodriguez did a better job. Mackenzie passed them all as she made her way back to the living room. There, she went to the little corner office. She powered up the laptop that was sitting on the corner desk and, as expected, was thwarted by a password screen.

"Well, there's some good news to come out of it all," Rodriguez said. "Moments before you guys stepped inside, I got a call from the precinct. Believe it or not, we have two Vaughans to look into."

"Both associated with swinger clubs?" Mackenzie asked as she looked through the well-organized papers and books on Decker's desk.

"Yeah," he said. "One appears to be a younger well-to-do couple and the other is a bit older. I had someone at the station speak with Gloria at DCM and she confirms that she has had dealings with both couples, though one had not been active for a while."

Mackenzie took all of this in as she looked through the assorted items around the desk. As she did so, Ellington spoke up over her shoulder. "I'll poke around the bedroom and see if I can find anything."

"I'll cover the bathroom," Nestler said.

Mackenzie could find nothing incriminating around the office area. Yet as she thumbed through one of the few books on his desk (a battered copy of what appeared to be a self-help book titled *It's Not All in Your Head*), an old Polaroid picture fell out. She picked it up and the blatant nature of what it showed shocked her. It was a picture of a woman's genitalia, but not shown in any sort of pornographic light. It was from very close up and obviously not taken by force.

She slid the picture back in and looked back to the password screen. She knew that, if necessary, she could have someone crack into it within a matter of minutes. But maybe it wouldn't come to that.

"Hey, Agent White?"

It was Nestler, calling from the bathroom.

"Yeah?" she asked, heading that way to join him.

"Your suspect supposedly has impotency issues, right?"

Before Mackenzie could respond, Nestler was coming out of the bathroom toward her. He tossed her a prescription bottle of pills. The script had Decker's name on it and was for a relatively high dose of a common drug to treat erectile dysfunction.

Definitely on the right track, she thought.

Another voice sounded out from the back of the house. This time, it was Ellington. "I've got a sort of gross jackpot back here," he called out.

Mackenzie went back to the master bedroom and saw that Ellington was standing by the bedside table. The table's single drawer was open; Ellington had taken several items out and spread them out on the bed.

Among the items were several photographs. These had been printed out on high-quality glossy photo paper. They were a little grainy, suggesting the pictures had been taken by a digital camera and then resized improperly. Still, the subject of the pictures was plain to see.

And quite haunting.

The four pictures showed four nude people. In some, two were on a bed while the other two surrounded it. The two on the bed were engaged in sex. Because the woman was on top and facing the camera, her face was clearly visible.

It was Vanessa Springs.

As for the two by the edge of the bed, the woman could not be clearly seen, as she was on her knees and facing away from the camera. The man she was servicing, though, was mostly visible. His head was arched up and looking away from the camera, but it was clearly Jack Springs.

She looked from picture to picture, trying to get a better look at the unseen man and woman. In one, she could see the reflection of the man in bed in a mirror to the right. The reflection in the grainy picture made it hard to be sure but it looked very much like a face she had seen quite recently in crime scene photos.

It was Josh Kurtz…leading Mackenzie to believe that the woman on her knees in front of Jack Springs was Julie.

"I wonder who is taking the pictures," Ellington said.

"The killer?" Rodriguez asked, looking over their shoulder.

"Possibly," Mackenzie said. "Either way, this confirms that Byron Decker was indeed connected to these two dead couples."

"And the Vaughans are the only other couple we know for sure was connected to him," Ellington added.

We need to get to them before the killer does, Mackenzie thought.

"We need to split up," she said. "Rodriguez, you take your team to one of the addresses and Ellington and I will go to the other one."

"Any preference?" he asked.

134

"No. Just text me the first one."

Rodriguez nodded and pulled out his phone to do just that. Mackenzie made her way to the door and stepped back outside. As they all filed out, Nestler tried his best to shut the door in a way where their forced entry wasn't so obvious.

"You feel good about this?" Ellington asked her as they got into the car.

"We have eight dead people," she said. "There's nothing good about this at all. I assume you're asking if I think we're about to track down our killer?"

"Yes, I am."

"In that case, yes…I think we do. Let's just hope we make it to the Vaughans before Decker does."

She cranked the car and pulled away from the curb.

It was 12:47 and she headed west, away from the beach that sat less than half a mile behind the house she had just forcibly entered. She went as fast as she could without being reckless.

And yet, even so, Mackenzie couldn't help but feel that they were probably already too late.

CHAPTER TWENTY EIGHT

Mackenzie could still feel the sense of urgency when she stepped out of the car. Still, she kept herself calm, forcing herself to get a proper lay of the land. The house was quite nice, one of the nicer ones in the neighborhood. It was a neighborhood very much like the one the Springses had lived in, only it was nearly on the other side of the city.

She looked up and down the streets and saw a few cars parked here and there. The closest one to them was an older model pickup truck. Two blocks down, a man was jogging, running in the opposite direction. Further off, she heard the buzz of a motorcycle engine. Otherwise, the street was basically dead.

One of the doors to the two-car garage was open. It revealed a large-bodied GMC truck. The tailgate was down and a series of clear empty plastic bags were stuffed into a corner.

"There's always the chance that these people work," Ellington said. "Like normal folks. It's Friday, after all."

"Possibly," Mackenzie said.

Yet as they made their way closer to the shallow front porch, Mackenzie started to doubt it. She saw mulch scattered here and there, as if accidentally dropped in the yard. *Probably from those empty bags in the back of the GMC,* she thought.

She then looked to the beautiful flower beds and saw that they were beautiful for a reason. They had recently been touched up. If the trowel and pair of gardening gloves sitting on the bottom porch step was any indication, it had been done *very* recently…as in, within the last couple of hours.

Mackenzie nodded toward the gloves and Ellington nodded. "There's a good chance someone is home," she said. "Did you see the truck?"

"In the garage. Yeah."

This yard work was done within the last few hours, she thought. *It seems like we got here before Decker. Hopefully we can—*

Someone screamed from inside the house. It was not a scream of pain, but one of surprise. This was followed by a voice that Mackenzie could barely hear. As this voice spoke, she also heard a slight thumping noise.

She raced to the door and knocked hard. Without waiting for a response, she yelled to whoever could hear her on the other side.

"I'm an FBI agent," she said loudly. "Mr. and Mrs. Vaughan, I'm coming."

She tried the door and found it locked.

Another scream sounded out from inside. This one was louder and, while not a pain-filled one, carried a lot of fear. She then heard loud footfalls and something falling over, shattering.

Then, as she stepped back to fire her gun at the locked doorknob, another scream came through the door.

"Help!"

Mackenzie raised her gun and fired a round into where she thought the lock was. Immediately following this, Ellington delivered a swift hard kick to the same place. The door went creaking open and Ellington gracefully brought his kick down and transformed it into a quick stride into the house.

Mackenzie followed him, again raising her gun. But she didn't even have time to assume a shooter's stance.

As Ellington cleared the doorway, a man came out of nowhere. He seemed to have been hiding behind the door itself, waiting for it come flying open. Mackenzie barely caught sight of the quick motion before the man collided with Ellington. The two men went tumbling back into the wall and when they struck, she heard Ellington let out a gasp of pain.

Mackenzie knew she would not get a clear shot without potentially hurting Ellington, so she reached out for the man's right arm.

That's when she saw the knife sticking out of Ellington's side.

It caused her just enough distraction to become defenseless for a split second. So while she *did* see the man's right hand come at her in a blinding fist and was able to draw her own hand up to block it, he had her beat. His right hand clipped her in the jaw and she stumbled backward, blinking back black stars that bloomed in her vision.

He came at her, his hands going for her throat, but Mackenzie started to raise her gun. He swatted at it, taking advantage of her temporary daze, and he did it with such force that it sent her spinning to the wall.

She waited for him to attack again, tensing herself up as she did her best to blink away the haze that had come over her from the sharp blow to her jaw.

Instead, she heard his footsteps. She also heard Ellington breathing heavy, now slumped to the floor to her right.

From somewhere else nearby, she heard a woman crying.

Mrs. Vaughan, she thought.

Mackenzie willed herself to her feet. She glanced to Ellington and saw that he had not lost a lot of blood, but he looked out of it.

The knife in his side was buried about four inches. She was no anatomy expert, but she knew that at the angle the blade was in and the location it was occupying, things were either going to be very bad for Ellington or he could potentially come out nearly unscathed.

She then wondered, almost morbidly, if the knife sticking out of him was the same knife that had been used to kill the four couples she had seen in the course of the last few days.

She got to her feet, shaking off the last of the haze from the punch. She saw the man that had attacked them heading for a large room ahead of them. He was heading for the living room, where Mackenzie saw the body for the first time.

It was a male, lying on his stomach. He was crawling forward, leaving streaks of blood on the light blue carpet. The attacker was heading for this man—having apparently already attacked him once.

Mackenzie sprinted toward him. He saw her out of the corner of his eye and turned to meet her. He drew back his fist just as she raised her gun. He charged her, hunkered down. She lowered her gun and fired a round. She then felt him strike her in the collarbone. It was not a hard punch but it sent a pins and needles sensation racing down her arm. Shocked, the arm went limp and she dropped her gun.

The attacker—the man she was now fairly certain was Byron Decker—then grabbed her by the shoulders and tried to throw a knee into her stomach. Instead, Mackenzie blocked his knee and grabbed his leg. She attempted to throw him over in a fireman's carry but her right arm was still tingling. So instead, they both went stumbling backward in an awkward little ball.

Decker released her and when he did, she sprang at him.

She realized her error too late.

She struck him hard and they went backward again, stumbling blindly.

She saw the sliding glass door behind them a moment before they crashed into it.

She felt the glass cutting into her about a split second after she heard it shattering all around them.

Suddenly, she was lying on her back on the Vaughans' back porch. She was staring up into the flawless blue sky and could already feel the stickiness of her own blood as it poured from her forearm and the back of her neck.

Somewhere beside her was the killer. And her gun. She had dropped the damned thing when she'd hit the wood of the porch.

She rolled over to locate Decker. Her left hand slid in the glass. It felt like dozens of insects biting her as tiny shards and splinters pierced her skin.

And then there he was—Byron Decker, standing over her with a large flower pot held over his head like a huge boulder, bringing it down to crack her skull.

CHAPTER TWENTY NINE

As Decker brought the flower pot down, Mackenzie lifted her leg and delivered as much strength as she could into a kick that landed squarely in the fork of his legs. His knees buckled and the pot went toppling to the patio. Mackenzie rolled to the right and dodged it, feeling yet more glass stick her exposed forearms and hands.

The pain wasn't too bad, honestly, but it seemed to be everywhere. She was bleeding enough so that she could actually smell it.

Worry about where you're hurt later, she told herself. *For now, get this asshole under control.*

Already, he was getting to his feet. The broken glass had done a number on him, too. His face was cut in four different places and a deep cut on the underside of his arm was dripping blood down to his hand and off of his fingers.

He threw a punch that she blocked easily. She then took the arm she had blocked and twisted it hard. He dropped to a knee right away, howling. As she pushed him forward and bent the arm further back, he used his other arm as a club of sorts. He drove his elbow into the meat of her upper thigh, causing her to stumble backward. The pain there was immense. She couldn't figure out why at first but then looked down and saw a shard of glass sticking out of her pants. The area was sticky with blood and she somehow hadn't even noticed it.

Apparently realizing that he was not going to win a fight against her, Decker made his way down the porch steps. He nearly fell in his escape, buying Mackenzie perhaps two whole seconds to push past the pain in her leg.

Realizing that she wouldn't be an effective runner with the wound in her leg (the glass still sticking out of it), she summoned up her strength, took one running stride, and then launched herself into the air just before she reached the first step.

Decker looked back just in time to see her before her full weight landed on his back. She fell on top of him and when he struck the ground she could literally feel the air leaving his lungs from the impact. He wiggled beneath her but a quick elbow between the shoulders put a stop to it.

She knew she had him under control but honestly just couldn't stop herself. With him pinned beneath her, his face planted into the ground, she delivered two vicious punches to his upper back. She heard the gasp as the wind flew out of him and a surge of pain raced through him.

She pinned his knees to the ground with her own knees, applying just enough pressure to ensure that any attempts at escape would hurt like hell. She then removed her cuffs from her belt and applied them as quickly as she could. When she realized that her hands were so sticky with her own blood that she nearly dropped the cuffs, she wondered if she might be hurt worse than she thought.

When Decker tried to fight her off when she went for his left arm, she grabbed it and wrenched it upward a little too hard. She grimaced, fully expecting to hear the snap of his forearm breaking. But she had stopped just in time. He cried out beneath her as she snapped the cuffs closed.

"Mackenzie…"

She turned and saw Ellington stumble out onto the porch. He had not removed the knife, likely knowing that to remove it could actually make matters worse.

"You okay?" she asked him.

"Don't know," he said. He looked to the porch stairs, seemed to consider walking down them, and then sat down hard. "Called it in," he said weakly. "You okay?"

"Yeah," she said, although she wasn't sure yet.

She was shaky as she got to her feet. Hauling Decker up was a feat in and of itself but she managed to do so, holding him firmly as he tried to buck against her.

"Don't even think about it," Ellington yelled weakly from the porch. "You get a few feet away from her, I'll take out your right knee."

Decker stopped then, hanging his head in defeat like a child that can't get its way.

"Up the stairs," Mackenzie said, nudging him along.

He didn't move. He remained in place and started to murmur something.

"I said get up the stairs," she said.

"If they aren't dead," he said, "then all of this was for nothing. The other eight meant absolutely nothing if the Vaughans aren't dead. I can't—"

"I said *move*," Mackenzie said.

She planted her foot squarely in his ass and shoved him forward. He tripped over the first step and fell down, nearly slamming his face into the stairs above him.

I hope he breaks his fucking nose, she thought.

"Get to your feet and get up the stairs," Mackenzie said as calmly as she could.

Decker obeyed, taking the steps slowly one by one. When they reached the top, Ellington weakly kicked Mackenzie's fallen sidearm out of their path so Decker couldn't possibly think of getting it.

Mackenzie did not like the look of Ellington. He was in shock. And there was more blood than she had seen about three minutes ago. It was starting to pool in his lap. He was trying to seem as coherent as possible, but she could tell it was a struggle.

Mackenzie picked up her Glock and trained it at Decker. "Inside," she spat.

Again, he obeyed. She was pretty sure he was weeping this time.

As she followed him inside, she knelt down by Ellington. She acted as if her only reason for doing so was to get his cuffs. While she had already slapped her own pair on Decker, she felt that she might need two if she would be holding Decker by herself. But she also knelt down in order to get a better look at Ellington. While he didn't look terrible, he was by no means well off.

"I'll return these," she said, trying to remain light-hearted. "You just hang in there."

"Yeah," Ellington said weakly, with an eye roll.

With that, she headed inside behind Decker to see just how much damage he had done before she and Ellington had arrived.

***

To ensure Decker was not able to try escaping while she investigated the house, Mackenzie would have to immobilize him. And she had no problem with that.

With her Glock still trained on him, she nodded toward the Vaughans' couch in the living room. "Sit," she said.

When he obeyed this command, he did so with an exaggerated sort of defeat. She was pretty sure she'd have no problems with him. While he sat, Mackenzie carefully knelt at his feet. She tensed up, waiting to block off any kicks or other attacks he might try. But he was completely docile as she snapped Ellington's cuffs around his ankles.

"Does it make you feel like you've achieved something?" he asked. "Arresting me. Beating me. Do you feel good about it?"

"Yeah, honestly," she said. "It feels pretty great."

He let out a maniacal little chuckle at this and started to stare at the floor. His eyes were drawn to the shattered glass he and Mackenzie had placed in the floor when crashing through the glass window.

There was so much she wanted to say to him but she didn't trust herself to try to speak to him civilly. So instead, she went back to the living room to look in on the man she had seen crawling in a pool of blood.

He had been sliced across the arm and there was a puncture wound in his chest. When he breathed, he made a wet sound that made Mackenzie cringe. As she knelt by him, knowing that the wife was somewhere in the house, she worried that she and Ellington had been too late.

The man's eyes coasted in her direction and she saw a faraway look there.

Thinking as quickly as she could, Mackenzie grabbed two dishtowels that were hanging from one of the cabinet handles in the kitchen. She pressed them to the man's chest, covering the wound. The blood instantly felt warm under her hands, even though the cloths.

"Can you press down on this?" she asked.

He nodded and took the cloths with one shaky hand. He pressed as hard as he could and let out a grunt of pain.

"Patricia," he said. "She…?"

"Hold on," Mackenzie said, not wanting leave his side.

She got up and turned, only to see a woman standing behind her. Her face was streaked with tears and there was blood on her white shirt. From what Mackenzie could tell, she was unharmed. But her wide eyes and rigid posture made Mackenzie think she was in a state of shock.

"Are you Patricia?" she asked.

The woman nodded.

"Patricia Vaughan?"

Again, another nod. She then took a deep shuddering breath as her eyes fell on her husband. Whatever fugue state she had been in crumbled in that moment. She nearly collapsed as she ran to him and let out a sob.

"Patricia," Mackenzie said. "I know it's difficult, but you need to stay off of him for now. We don't know how badly he's hurt."

Patricia stopped inches away from him. She reached out and took his hand. Mackenzie felt the smallest flicker of hope when she saw that he had enough strength to squeeze his wife's hand.

"Patricia, I know it's scary, but I need you to try to speak with me. Police and an ambulance are on their way and we can't do much of anything until then. So do you think you can answer some quick questions?"

"Yes, yeah...I...what happened?"

"How did this man get into your house?" she asked, nodding back toward where Decker was still double-cuffed on the couch.

"He knocked," Patricia answered. "We know him—from a while back. He was apologizing for something he did a few years ago. He seemed genuinely sorry, started crying. So we let him in. And as soon as the door was closed...he...he pulled out the knife and attacked Henry. I tried to help but I was in shock, I think, couldn't move, couldn't..."

The sound of approaching sirens distracted her. The noise seemed to bring on a whole new level of anxiety. Rather than relieving her by knowing that help was on the way, the blaring commotion from outside seemed to alert Patricia even more to the fact that her husband was in serious trouble.

Maybe Ellington, too, she thought. She desperately wanted to run out to him but for right now, the Vaughans had to be her first priority.

"Patricia...are you hurt?"

"No," she said. "The blood on my shirt is Henry's...you came in and saved us...just in time. Thank you."

And with that, Patricia lost it. She crumpled up and started bawling. By her side, Henry did his best to comfort her by saying her name but he wasn't able to use his voice—more like a garbled sound of pain and blood.

When Mackenzie heard the screeching of tires and slamming doors out front, she raced to Ellington. Moving at such a speed reminded her that she wasn't in tip-top shape, either. The wound in her upper thigh was stinging and throbbing. The underside of her palm felt raw where tiny shards of glass had punctured and rubbed her skin.

On the back porch, she saw that Ellington had mustered the strength to get to his feet. He was currently leaning against the side of the house, looking like he might get sick at any moment.

"How bad is it?" she asked.

"Hurts like a bitch. Seems to feel better when I'm standing. Starting to feel a little dizzy but I think I'll be okay."

"Help just arrived," she said.

144

He nodded and closed his eyes. She could tell that he was trying his absolute best to not let her know that he was in a great deal of pain.

"You did good," he said. "This is on me. I shouldn't have gone in so fast, so hard. I shouldn't have—"

"Shut up," she said. "Save your strength."

He nodded and let out a groan. Mackenzie took one more look at the knife still sticking out of his side and realized just how risky of a situation it was. Until the knife was out and he was properly attended to, there was no telling how much damage had been done.

She heard the front door open and she started forward as paramedics and police came filing in. She made it two steps toward the shattered glass door before Ellington stopped her.

"Hey...I know you're like a superhero and all and want to be in there...but is it selfish of me to ask you to stay with me?"

She couldn't suppress her smile. He was right. She *did* feel the need to get inside and help in any way she could. But she also *did* want to stay there with him.

She walked over to him and took his hand. She felt him trembling beneath her touch, his body responding in the only way it knew how to the trauma it was enduring.

She stayed by his side, his hand in hers, until the first of the paramedics stepped out onto the back porch.

CHAPTER THIRTY

The afternoon was a sea of chaos for Mackenzie. She stayed with Ellington as long as she could. She rode to the hospital in the back of an ambulance with him. He was coherent the entire time but there were a few occasions where he seemed to be on the verge of passing out. By the time they arrived at the hospital and he was admitted, the news the medics were able to give her wasn't as bad as it could have been, but it wasn't anything trivial, either.

The knife had grazed one of his ribs. Had it not, it would have punctured his lung. There was still a chance that there was a minor puncture that would not be found until a more thorough examination could be conducted.

While she waited for news on Henry Vaughan and Ellington, she received her own treatment. She spent two hours being seen by doctors, getting four stitches in the side of her right hand and eight in her thigh. The ones in her thigh hurt like hell but she toughed her way through it. Getting the shards of glass removed from her forearms was no picnic, either.

Still, she was cleared and bandaged up by five o'clock that afternoon. She received word that Ellington was in the clear, though he'd obviously be getting stitches and would be off of his feet for a while.

As for Henry Vaughan, he was a case of touch-and-go. Upon arriving at the hospital, early indications suggested he would not make it through the evening. Then, by the time Mackenzie had been cleared, he was showing promising signs of pulling through.

Before leaving the hospital, Mackenzie walked by Ellington's room. She took a step inside but saw that he was sleeping. She stood in the doorway for a moment and marveled at how strange life was. She'd come to Miami with Harrison, with Ellington nothing more than a sizeable speck on her radar. And now, after just a few days, things were very much different. Now, she could have easily remained in his room, sitting there only to watch him, until he stirred awake.

But he'd make fun of her for that, and rightfully so.

Besides…while they had caught their killer, the case wasn't quite over. She had somewhere else to be. And if Ellington's injury was going to be worth something, it was her duty to go.

With one last fond look at Ellington, Mackenzie left the hospital and headed to the precinct.

When she stepped through the front doors, there was a stifling sort of silence as the few people in the lobby noticed her arrival. Then something surreal happened. People started to applaud. She'd seen this sort of thing in movies and had heard a few stories while in the academy of this sort of thing happening. But it was weird to have it happen to her—especially when she felt that it was not deserved.

She gave a few vague smiles as she made her way back to Rodriguez's office. As she had expected, it was empty. She veered further down the hallway toward the interrogation rooms—a part of their building that she was getting far too familiar with.

She bypassed the interrogation room and headed for the door to the observation room. She knocked and the door was answered by Nestler. He ushered her in quickly, with the same look of appreciation on his face that she had seen in the lobby from the workers and scattered officers.

Dagney and two other officers she had not yet met were also in the room. They were looking through the glass, where Decker and Rodriguez occupied the room on the other side.

"How long has he been at it?" Mackenzie asked.

"About twenty minutes," Nestler said. "But we've had Decker in there for about an hour and a half."

"I think Rodriguez might not mind you joining him," Dagney added.

Mackenzie nodded, studying Byron Decker through the glass. He looked weak and tired. He sat slouched, his shoulder hunched and his head hanging low. She slowly made her way out of the room and walked to the interrogation room. She knocked and then opened the door, poking her head in.

"Am I okay to come in?" she asked.

Rodriguez seemed slightly relieved to see her. He nodded and waved her in. Decker looked up at her and then directly back down into his lap. There was a bandage on his forehead and an entire wrap around his forearm. The afternoon had been so hectic and violent that she had nearly forgotten that Decker had taken a beating, too—not just from her, but from the sliding glass door.

Rodriguez sidled up next to her and whispered into her ear. "He's not being confrontational. He wants to talk, I think. He's already admitted to killing the four couples and attempting to kill the Vaughans. He's cooperative, just...not all there."

Mackenzie stepped toward the table. Decker still didn't look up at her.

"Mr. Decker...after I handcuffed you, you started to weep. And now you won't even look up at either one of us. Are you embarrassed that you were caught?"

He shook his head. "No. I'm embarrassed, but not that I was caught. That was inevitable. Even if I had made it to Juarez...I would have been caught. I knew that the instant I decided to do this. And that was a turn-on. It was the biggest turn-on of this whole thing. Except for killing Vanessa Springs. *That* was erotic as hell."

"What's in Juarez, Mr. Decker?"

He grew silent.

Through the haze of tears she saw the insanity lurking. Maybe not even insanity, but evil. She did believe true evil existed and that in some cases, it resided in humans.

She thought she'd try a new tack.

"You killed those couples because you felt slighted, didn't you?" she asked.

He didn't reply for a long time. Then, finally, he said, in a small voice, "I was ridiculed. Mocked."

She breathed deep, trying to contain her rage.

"And that was cause enough for those people to die? Because you couldn't get it up?"

Anger flashed in his eyes but he swallowed it down like a snake. He smirked at her. "You'd be a hit at one of those clubs. I know a few men that would do what I've done this past week for a chance to get at you. You know that?"

She reddened with rage.

"I'm not exactly flattered," she said. "Mr. Decker...where was your wife in all of this?"

Decker looked up, surprised that she didn't already know. "She started it with me...the swinging. But we stopped when my wife started having an affair and left me. I couldn't...I couldn't please her sexually."

"So you kept trying to be a part of those swinging environments after she left, right?"

He fell silent again.

Finally, he shook his head. "You'll never understand."

She left the room in a hurry, feeling a series of emotions similar to the ones that had sent her quickly out of the room before.

What the hell is wrong with me?

She stood outside the interrogation room, drawing in a series of deep breaths. Rodriguez came out, clearly unsure of how to approach her.

"Are you okay?" he asked.

"I will be," she said.

"I can't thank you enough for what you and your partner have done. Unless there is anything pressing you need to handle here, I encourage you to sign off. Go get some rest. Check in on your partner. We've got it covered here. I'll be calling your director and letting him know what a fine job you've done here."

"Thank you."

With that, she took his advice. She headed back outside to her car. She thought about calling McGrath to fill him in. She'd spoken to him once already today while waiting to get her stitches. He'd requested that she remain in Miami until Ellington was well enough to come back with her.

She headed back toward the hospital, irritated by the itch and slight sting of the stitches in her thigh and hand. Yet she glanced out of the window and saw the palm trees on every corner and the slice of blue afternoon sky giving way to the purple of twilight and felt a sense of peace.

Miami certainly had its share of beauty, but she sure as hell wasn't going to miss it.

CHAPTER THIRTY ONE

As it turned out, Ellington was cleared to leave the hospital at 8:30 the following morning. Mackenzie received the news after being tapped awake in the chair of his hospital room, as the doctor smiled down at her warmly.

Ellington showed no signs of infection and though there was a bit of minor scarring on the surface of his lung, there had been no puncture or real damage. Barring a checkup in one week in D.C., it seemed like he had come out of the encounter with Byron Decker very lucky.

There was a comfortable silence between them as the very slow discharge process was carried out. She filled him on the interrogation of Decker at the precinct as best as she could. The last update she'd received had come the night before, when Rodriguez had called her to let her know that everything was basically over, wrapped up with a bow. Decker wasn't even trying to deny any of what he had done; more than that, he had started to go into detail about how he had planned it all out.

When Ellington stepped into the bathroom to slip out of his hospital robe and into his street clothes, Mackenzie saw the wound where the knife had gone in. The doctors had done a beautiful job on the stitch work but it was hidden by a double layer of gauze. Seeing it made Mackenzie uneasy. Another inch deeper and the knife could have harmed him very badly. It might even have killed him.

I've spent far too much time in hospital rooms lately, she thought. Sadly, an image of Bryers in his hospital room came to her mind. She couldn't help but smile, though. He'd be proud of her for managing to wrap this case, saving the Vaughans and bringing a killer to justice.

When he came back out, he was dressed in jeans and a Washington Redskins T-shirt. The doctors had suggested he wear sweatpants, mesh shorts, or some other elastic and forgiving material while he healed. Having none of those packed in his suitcase, he had to settle for jeans.

"I thought about not buttoning them, just to keep them loose against me," he said as he came out of the bathroom, tapping at his jeans. "But I didn't want to tease you. Looks like I'm out of commission for a while."

"That's a shame," she said. It was a half-hearted joke, but she actually meant it.

"You know," he said, "I'm not a fan of stretchy pants or shorts, but I think I have an idea. Would you humor me?"

She gave him a playfully skeptical grin as they headed for the door of his hospital room. "I'm not quite sure how to process that question."

"Just trust me," he said, taking her hand as if it was the most natural thing in the world.

Hand in hand, they headed out of his room.

Just trust me, he said.

Mackenzie was a little taken aback to realize that she did—unflinchingly and without question.

***

The idea he'd had was childlike and a little irresponsible, but Mackenzie went along with it anyway. Between the hospital and the motel, they stopped at a little mom and pop surf shop where Ellington purchased a pair of painfully bright swim trunks. When they were back at the motel, he changed into them, needing Mackenzie's help to balance himself as he slipped his jeans off and put the trunks on. Mackenzie then loaded up their suitcases while Ellington settled up the room bills.

It took less than two minutes for them to reach a beach outlet. Ellington had to walk very slowly down the wooden walkway that led out onto the beach. She noticed him grunting as they made their way down the steps and into the sand. A hundred yards or so ahead of them, waves crashed along the beach. Gulls swooped down, crying out to one another. To their left, a few kids were throwing a Frisbee in the shallow water, dancing around the waves.

It was the same stretch of beach Mackenzie had come to when she'd been working on her laptop. They found the same bench she'd sat on; it was unoccupied although there was wet towel draped over it, left behind and forgotten by a beachgoer.

As they sat down, Ellington gazed out to the ocean with the awe of a child. "You like the beach?" he asked.

"I was indifferent for most of my life," she said. "But something about this case is drawing me to it. It's sort of peaceful in a chaotic way."

"Sounds like the basis of my life," Ellington said. He sighed and looked at his watch. "Any idea when the next flight to DC is?" he asked.

"I haven't looked into it yet. I'll check it out in a minute."

He nodded, still staring at the ocean. "Mackenzie...the other night was amazing. And there's not a part of me that doesn't regret it. But I know you...I know your work ethic. If you think it's going to get in your way or interfere, then I—"

She interrupted him with a kiss. It was slow, passionate, and deliberate. When she broke it, she smiled sweetly at him. "I'm not thinking about it," she said. "I'm just letting it be what it is for right now."

Ellington thought about this for a moment but then nodded his agreement.

"I'm sorry I snapped at you yesterday morning," she said. "About my dad. That whole thing...it has a hook in me, deeper than I realized. But I'm working on it."

"It's okay. I get it. It's personal. It hurts."

"Yeah, that's all true. But...well, there have been developments. Very recent developments. And I'm tired of internalizing it all. I'm going to tell you all of it, if you want to hear it."

"Right now?"

"Yeah, I think so."

He seemed at ease with it. He was no longer staring out to the ocean. He was now staring at her, giving her that same rapt attention.

And so she told him everything. She started with a young girl in Nebraska, walking into her parents' bedroom and finding her father dead, with a gunshot wound to the head. She ended with the discovery of a business card at a more recent scene—a card reading **Barker Antiques**. With each word, Mackenzie could feel the weight coming off of her. It was freeing. It was like having an exorcism performed and feeling some other nasty presence expelling itself from her.

At some point, he took her hand in his and it made the telling easier.

She looked from Ellington and then to the ocean. Something about the waves made her feel like a child again. She felt as if with every moment of her story she got out, the waves would wash it away and pull it back out to the sea, never to be seen again.

But that was a silly hope.

She'd told Ellington that her past had hooks in her and that was undeniably true. The hooks went deep and, from time to time, they stung quite badly.

But as she shared the story of her father's case and the current progress with it being reopened, she felt as if maybe, just maybe, one day she might be able to remove them once and for all.

BEFORE HE FEELS
(A Mackenzie White Mystery—Book 6)

From Blake Pierce, bestselling author of ONCE GONE (a #1 bestseller with over 900 five star reviews), comes book #6 in the heart-pounding Mackenzie White mystery series.

In BEFORE HE FEELS (A Mackenzie White Mystery—Book 6), FBI special agent Mackenzie White is stunned to be assigned a case with victims matching no profile she has ever seen: shockingly, all of the victims are blind.

Does this mean that the killer himself is blind, too?

Plunged into the subculture of the blind, Mackenzie struggles to understand, finding herself out of her element as she crisscrosses the state, racing from group homes to private houses, interviewing caretakers, librarians, experts and psychologists.

And yet, despite the best minds in the country, Mackenzie seems unable to prevent the spree of killings.

Has she finally met her match?

A dark psychological thriller with heart-pounding suspense, BEFORE HE FEELS is book #6 in a riveting new series—with a beloved new character—that will leave you turning pages late into the night.

Blake Pierce

Blake Pierce is author of the bestselling RILEY PAGE mystery series, which includes eight books (and counting). Blake Pierce is also the author of the MACKENZIE WHITE mystery series, comprising five books (and counting); of the AVERY BLACK mystery series, comprising four books (and counting); and of the new KERI LOCKE mystery series.

An avid reader and lifelong fan of the mystery and thriller genres, Blake loves to hear from you, so please feel free to visit www.blakepierceauthor.com to learn more and stay in touch.

BOOKS BY BLAKE PIERCE

RILEY PAIGE MYSTERY SERIES
ONCE GONE (Book #1)
ONCE TAKEN (Book #2)
ONCE CRAVED (Book #3)
ONCE LURED (Book #4)
ONCE HUNTED (Book #5)
ONCE PINED (Book #6)
ONCE FORSAKEN (Book #7)
ONCE COLD (Book #8)
ONCE STALKED (Book #9)

MACKENZIE WHITE MYSTERY SERIES
BEFORE HE KILLS (Book #1)
BEFORE HE SEES (Book #2)
BEFORE HE COVETS (Book #3)
BEFORE HE TAKES (Book #4)
BEFORE HE NEEDS (Book #5)
BEFORE HE FEELS (Book #6)

AVERY BLACK MYSTERY SERIES
CAUSE TO KILL (Book #1)
CAUSE TO RUN (Book #2)
CAUSE TO HIDE (Book #3)
CAUSE TO FEAR (Book #4)

KERI LOCKE MYSTERY SERIES
A TRACE OF DEATH (Book #1)
A TRACE OF MUDER (Book #2)
A TRACE OF VICE (Book #3)

Made in the USA
Monee, IL
15 July 2020